THE **SECRET** OF HUNTER'S BOG

ALLY BLUE

RIPTIDE
PUBLISHING

Riptide Publishing
PO Box 1537
Burnsville, NC 28714
www.riptidepublishing.com

The Secret of Hunter's Bog

Cover art: Kanaxa, kanaxa.com
Editor: Delphine Dryden, delphinedryden.com/editing
Layout: L.C. Chase, lcchase.com/design.htm

ISBN: 978-1-62649-374-2

First edition
March, 2016

Also available in ebook:
ISBN: 978-1-62649-373-5

THE SECRET OF HUNTER'S BOG

ALLY BLUE

RIPTIDE
PUBLISHING

This book is lovingly dedicated to Del, Sarah, and all the ladies in the Chicago Cab Ride of October 2014, because that's where this whole idea was born. Thank you for being inspirational and enabling :)

TABLE OF CONTENTS

CHAPTER 1

"**T**here it is, in all its dubious glory." Koichi McNab surveyed the brand-new space where he and his twin sister, Kimmy, were getting ready to reopen the family business. The place was bland as custard, but it was four walls and a roof. A big display window, even, with the shop's name already painted on it. He wrinkled his nose. "It'll do, I guess."

Kimmy waved one hand in a dismissive gesture. "Stop being such a grump. It's fine."

He cut her an *oh, please* look, which she ignored. They both knew the strip mall wasn't an ideal spot for McNab's Organic Home Goods. But it was newly built and clean, and the rent was cheap. Besides, after their old place in downtown Duchene had burned down, this was the only space available—unless they wanted to run their business out of Koichi's house, or move the shop ten miles north to the next closest town, Bay Minette.

Koichi sidestepped away from thinking of the fire. He'd escaped by the skin of his teeth with nothing worse than a small burn on his arm, but the real scars were the invisible ones.

"Yeah. Fine." Koichi patted the cowlick at the back of his head, where his hair always stuck straight up no matter how hard he tried to make it lie down. "Well, like Mama said, it's a place, right? It'll grow on me." *I seriously fucking hope.*

Laughing, Kimmy hooked her delicate little hand through Koichi's elbow. "She told you to quit bitching and be grateful we had the old building insured enough to replace our stock and rent this new place."

Guilt stabbed Koichi in the gut, like it did pretty much all the time. The whole family kept telling him he had nothing to prove—that the fire was an accident, and no one blamed him—but he knew better. He saw how they all gave him the side eye when they thought he wasn't looking.

"Right." With a deep sigh, he peered into her upturned face. "Shall we, sister of mine?"

She tossed her long black ponytail over her narrow shoulder. "Oh, let's."

Together, as they'd been their whole lives, they sauntered into their new shop.

It took another couple of weeks to get everything in order for their opening. They were lucky. Lots of the tenants of the new Hunter's Bog Mall took much longer to get ready, mostly because they were newbies. New to Alabama, particularly to the rapidly developing countryside north of Fairhope and south of Bay Minette.

"I don't think any of these guys have the slightest idea how to run a business," Koichi observed as he and Kimmy arranged homemade soaps, detergents, and other products on their locally sourced wooden shelves.

Kimmy shook her head. "I don't know what makes you think so. I was talking with Margie Sullivan yesterday. You know, the lady who's opening the nail salon? She's got a solid business plan."

"She's an exception, then." He placed the last bar of handmade goat's milk soap on the display and stepped back to examine his work. "These people are *way* too excited to be in a stupid strip mall next to a swamp. We're not gonna do as well here as we did in town."

"You don't know that. It's not like we ever got anything other than local trade in downtown Duchene." She studied the display of beeswax-and-honey lip balms beside the register and started rearranging them for at least the third time. "Hell, we might do *better* here. At least we're on the main road. That means tourists, Chichi."

He cast her a sharp look. Her face revealed nothing. He couldn't tell if she was just trying to make him feel better about the fire or not.

She'd done a lot of that ever since it had happened. Which was sweet and annoying at the same time.

In any case, she had a point. Anyone who visited the tiny town of Duchene had to do it on purpose, since it was off the beaten path. Hunter's Bog Mall, on the other hand, sat on the main highway running along the Eastern Shore from the Gulf of Mexico all the way into the Alabama interior. Which meant the new mall had good business potential. Historically, the Gulf and the quaint little towns along Mobile Bay's Eastern Shore had always been the big draw for tourists and transplants alike. But lately people had started to discover the excellent kayaking and fishing available along Alabama's southeastern rivers, which meant more tourist dollars in the Duchene area.

On the other hand, they'd had a steady stream of customers at their old shop; locals who'd been buying from their family store for decades, ever since Grammy McNab opened it fifty years ago. Koichi worried over how much trade they might lose with this forced move. Tourist dollars were great, but that money wasn't as dependable as local business.

A soft *thump* startled him out of his thoughts. He turned in a circle, but saw nothing out of place. Frowning, he crossed the shop and stuck his head into the storeroom in the back. All the boxes still seemed to be where he and Kimmy had put them.

"Hey, Kimmy?" he called.

"Yeah?"

"Did you hear that?"

"What?"

"That thump. A few seconds ago." Outside, beyond the open back door and the employee parking lot, Hunter's Bog stretched out as far as he could see. The mist that shrouded the swamp every morning was gone, and the afternoon sun drenched the dreary place in a warm golden light. It was pretty in a sad, bedraggled sort of way. "I thought it came from in the shop, or maybe the storeroom, but I don't see anything out of order."

"It's probably the ghost."

He jumped at Kimmy's voice right behind him. "Damn it, Kimmy."

She cackled as he turned to glare at her. "I scared you, huh?"

"You wish."

"I *know*."

He sighed. "So, did you hear that thump?"

"Yeah." She gave him a look suggesting he'd asked something unforgivably stupid. "I told you, it's probably the ghost." She brushed past him, went to the shelves along the wall, and picked up a box of sage bundles. "You *do* know the bog's haunted, right?"

"I've heard the stories." Who hadn't? It was a local legend: countless hunters over the years had gone missing in Hunter's Bog, and their restless spirits now haunted the twelve-plus square miles of stunted trees, tall reeds, and winding waterways beside which the developers had inexplicably decided to build a strip mall. "Even if I believed that, which you know I don't, why would the swamp ghosts be making thumping noises in the building? That's weird, even for a ghost."

Kimmy switched paths without missing a beat. "Could be our new neighbor. He's got a crap-load of heavy stuff over there."

Well, that made more sense, anyway. Koichi followed his sister out of the storeroom and back into the shop. "I didn't know that space was rented yet. What's in there?"

"Hood's Luxury Outdoor Expeditions & Supplies."

He laughed. "Wow. That's a mouthful."

"I know, right?" She set the box of sage on the floor below her display of herbs and started unpacking. "He's gonna be taking people glamping."

Koichi had heard of the glamour camping trend, but he didn't get it. You could dress up a tent however much you wanted, but it was still a tent. In his opinion, tents were for when civilization ended and all the hotels were gone.

He took several bundles of sage from the box and handed them to Kimmy to arrange on the display. "There's enough weirdos out there that he'll probably make a killing." The *thump* came again, this time definitely from the other side of the wall they shared with the glamping place. It was followed by a squeak, like someone moving furniture. "There it goes again. I guess it's not any ghost after all."

"Guess not." Kimmy gave him a sly glance as she moved herbs around, stacking some on the raised shelf and laying others on the counter below it. "You should go over there."

"I don't camp, sis."

"Oh my God, don't pretend to be stupid. Go say hello, okay? Be neighborly." The loudest thump yet rattled Kimmy's rack of essential oils. "Maybe help him move some of that shit before he knocks a hole in the wall."

Koichi watched his sister with thirty-three years' worth of well-earned suspicion. "What're you up to?"

"Huh?" She glanced at him, all wide green eyes and false innocence. "Why would I be up to something?"

"Don't give me that. We shared a womb." He crossed his arms and stared at her while she draped a sparkly scarf over the metal frame at the back of the shelf. "Are you trying to set me up again?"

She tried to hide the quick flash of guilt in her eyes, but she wasn't fast enough. He sighed. "Goddamn it, Kimmy."

She threw both hands in the air. "I'm not trying to set you up, okay? I just think you ought to make more of an effort to meet people." She stared at the floor, shoulders hunched. "We've had this place for weeks now. We've been over here several times. I've met almost all the other owners, but you haven't talked to one single person."

Shit. She was right. Not that it made him any more eager to go make friends. "I'm sorry I accused you, sis. And I know I haven't been friendly or anything, but . . ." He sighed. "It's hard for me. You know that."

"I know." She raised her head. Her eyes glittered with compassion and frustration. "Look, I totally get that you're more of an introvert than me. That's fine. And believe me, I *know* what a rough time you had growing up here. It wasn't always easy for me either. But we're not kids anymore. Sometimes you just gotta put yourself out there."

Resentment flared through Koichi's blood, dying out as fast as it rose. He couldn't stay mad at Kimmy just because she didn't understand what growing up gay in rural Alabama was like, or because she didn't get that his adult experiences had shaped him every bit as much as his childhood had.

"Sis, I love you more than anyone else in the world. And I seriously appreciate you standing by me ever since . . ." He swallowed, his throat tight. He still had a hard time talking about it. "You know. The fire."

Her expression softened. "Chichi—"

He cut her off before she could tell him any comforting lies. "You're right, okay? I need to get out there more. But I need to do it in my own time. Can you understand that?"

"Yeah, of course." Next door, something heavy hit the floor, followed by an eloquent stream of curses. "For now, could you please go help that poor guy with his stuff? I'm seriously afraid he's gonna either break something, or hurt himself."

Part of him resisted the idea of going. He vividly remembered the time he'd mustered the courage to speak to the friendly-looking boy at the desk next to his in ninth-grade algebra, only to be jumped by that boy and two of his friends on the way home from school that afternoon. He still had two crowns from the broken teeth.

On the other hand, the guy next door really did seem to be in danger of causing damage to either the building, his inventory, or his spine.

"All right," he said. "I'll go help out, for you, and for the integrity of this building."

She grinned as if she knew all the things he thought but hadn't said, which she probably did. "Thank you, Chichi." Abandoning the herb display, she took his hands in hers and kissed his cheek. "You're my favorite brother. Love you."

He laughed. She used that line all the time, since he was the only boy out of the five siblings. "I'll be back in a bit."

"If you don't come back, I'll assume you've become ensnared by his masculine wiles."

Christ almighty. "Bye, Kimmy."

Leaving his sister to her herbs, he walked out into the April sunshine and stopped outside the smoked-glass door marked *Hood's Luxury Outdoor Expeditions & Supplies*. Inside, a tall, broad-shouldered man in faded jeans and nothing else was lifting a long metal rack into place on the wall. The muscles in his arms and back stood out hard and firm. The only bit Koichi could see of his face was part of a jaw, but it seemed tight, as if his features were set in a grimace.

The rack was obviously too long for one person to hang alone. Once it was up, it would take up half of one wall. No wonder there'd been so much noise over here. It must've fallen more than once. Koichi felt bad for him, that he didn't have anyone to help him.

Speaking of which, he also felt kind of bad for standing there ogling the guy instead of going in to offer him a hand, since that was why he'd come over in the first place. But hell, what sort of normal person could manage *not* to stare? That body was fucking *gorgeous*.

As if he'd heard Koichi drooling, the man turned his head and nearly dropped the rack again when his gaze caught Koichi's. Embarrassed, Koichi waved through the window. "Need help?" he called.

Mister Hot Stuff blinked a couple of times like he was trying to clear his vision, then hollered back. "It's unlocked. C'mon in."

Here goes nothing. Putting on his friendliest smile, Koichi pushed the door open and went in.

On this side of the glass, his neighbor's struggle with the heavy rack seemed a lot more urgent, his breathing heavy and a tremor running through his arms. Those beautifully muscular arms . . . Mmmmm . . .

Focus, Koichi.

He hurried over, took hold of the sagging end of the rack, and lifted it. "Hi. I'm Koichi McNab, from McNab's Organic Home Goods next door."

Hot Stuff grinned, brown eyes sparkling. "Will Hood. Good to meet you. Thanks for rescuing me."

"No problem." A drop of sweat trickled from Will's armpit and ran down his side. Koichi ordered himself not to watch it meander south toward the jeans clinging to Will's sharp hip bones. That way madness lay. "So. Uh. What're we doing here?"

"I just need to get this stupid thing in the brackets. I can't seem to get it by myself."

"Okay. Say when."

"On three."

Will counted, and the two of them heaved the heavier-than-it-looked rack into place. Even working together, it was a tougher job

ALLY BLUE

than Koichi would've thought. They each had to push their end of the rack down into the tight brackets at the same time to keep one end or the other from sliding loose.

Once they were done, Koichi wiped sweat from his brow with the tail of his T-shirt. "Damn. No wonder you couldn't do it by yourself. That thing's a real bitch."

"No kidding." Will peered at him with those big, dark, long-lashed eyes and smiled. "Thanks, Koichi. I probably would've been here all day trying to get that done if you hadn't come by to help."

"My pleasure." Koichi felt himself returning Will's smile. He knew he looked goofy, because he always did when faced with a good-looking man. And damn, but Will Hood was seriously cute, with his little-boy grin and tousled brown hair falling into his ridiculously pretty eyes. "Is there anything else you need help with? As long as I'm here, I mean."

I promise not to lick you. Or sniff your crotch. Koichi kept those things behind his teeth where they belonged. Though to be fair, he wasn't sure if he was being polite, or if he simply didn't want to make promises he wasn't positive he could keep.

Biting his plump bottom lip in a most fetching way, Will cast a worried look at the wall he shared with McNab's Organics. "You sure you don't need to get back and help Kimmy?"

For half a second, Koichi was thrown for a loop. Then he remembered his sister had already been over here.

He put on an unconcerned expression and dismissed Kimmy with a wave of his hand. "Naw, she's fine. I'll just be in her way at this point."

Which might even be true. She liked the displays a certain way, and had an annoying habit of rearranging arrangements he'd already arranged. Might as well let her do it the way she wanted from the get-go and save them both the aggravation.

Will's smile returned, wider than before. "Well, if Kimmy's okay with it." He scratched his long fingers through his hair, making it even more perfectly ruffled. How in the hell did he do that? Did he just fall out of bed looking like a fucking model? Wow. "I have some more shelves to put up, and a glam tent to raise in the corner over there. I'd sure appreciate the help."

8

"It's settled, then. I'm all yours." Koichi spread his arms wide, beaming, as if his skinny ass was some sort of prize.

"Fantastic. Thank you." Will turned and marched his hot self into the back of the shop. "C'mon. We'll grab the tent and get that set up first."

Koichi swallowed. Hellfire and damnation, as Grammy would say.

He followed Will into the storeroom.

CHAPTER 2

Will watched Koichi on the sly while the two of them set up the tent. He couldn't help it. Koichi was slim and graceful, with a lovely Cupid's bow mouth, and the way his midnight-black hair stuck up in the back made Will's heart thump for reasons he couldn't explain. But it was his eyes that truly commanded attention: almond-shaped and green as spring leaves, with an intensity that pierced like needles and left Will feeling naked.

Discomfort squirmed in Will's belly. He hadn't come to Alabama looking for a man. Well, in point of fact, he had. But so far, that particular man had proven elusive. And he hadn't seen Anthony in a couple of years, which put this whole adventure on shaky ground from the start.

What was wrong with looking at an attractive guy, anyway? He was only human. And Koichi was awfully cute.

"Will?"

Startled, he shook himself out of his thoughts. Not literally. He hoped. "Hmm? Yeah?"

Koichi's lips curved into the half-sweet, half-devilish grin that had been screwing with Will's head ever since his neighbor had walked through the door. "What do I do with this?" Koichi held up a curtain made of embroidered blue-gray silk, so large it hid him from view and puddled on the floor.

"Oh. That's a tent divider." Will lifted the heavy material from Koichi's hands, accidentally-on-purpose letting their fingers brush together. An unmistakable heat flared in those brilliant green eyes for a second. Grinning, Will bent and picked up the bag of sturdy, rustproof metal rings from the floor. "C'mon. We'll hang it up. It looks a lot nicer than one of those zip-up nylon walls."

He got a husky laugh in answer. "I'll bet." Koichi followed him into the canvas tent, which was set up now but not yet furnished. "So. Glamping, huh?"

"Yep." He sat on the floor and set the bag of curtain rings beside him. "You want to start on one end and I'll start on the other? We'll get done in half the time that way."

"Sure." Koichi plopped onto the floor beside him, watched him work for a moment, then started popping rings into place with near-perfect technique. "I've never been into camping, myself. If I'm away from home, I'd prefer a four-star hotel."

Will laughed. "Spoiled."

"You sound like my sister."

"I like your sister."

"You and the rest of the world." Koichi cast him a coy glance from under his lashes. "She's gonna be after you to take her camping. Just so you know. She *loves* camping."

Will barely managed not to bounce in place like a moron. He could imagine having a wonderful time camping with Kimmy. "Hey, she can come with me anytime. I'd love that."

Koichi wrinkled his nose. "Y'all have fun."

Damn, he was cute. Will wanted to pounce on him and give him hickeys, but that might not go over so well. "I bet I could convert you. To glamping, I mean."

Pfft, went Koichi. "Bet you can't."

"Is that a challenge?" Will had never been able to resist a challenge. Especially when it came to convincing skeptics of the joys of glamping.

Koichi tilted his head sideways, studying Will as if he couldn't decide what to think of him. Which was probably true. "Depends. Are you up to that level of challenge?"

And thus, the gauntlet was thrown.

Will leveled his most intimidating stare at Mister Smart Mouth. "Oh, I'm up to it, McNab. I'll pamper your four-star-hotel ass off. And you'll *like* it."

"You're on, Hood." Flashing that troublemaking grin again, Koichi held out his hand. "Shake on it."

Will took Koichi's hand in his, and they shook.

The shop door opened with a rush of traffic noise from outside. "Hello? Where're y'all at?"

Kimmy. Will let go of Koichi's hand and scrambled to his feet. "We're in here. In the tent."

He heard Kimmy snicker. "Okay, then."

"Jesus Christ, sis, get your mind out of the gutter." With a swift, apologetic glance at Will, Koichi stood and strode out into the shop. Will followed him.

Kimmy grinned at them both. "Sorry. But, I mean, c'mon. You can forgive me, right?"

"Um." Will shuffled his feet, embarrassed.

Koichi gave his twin a playful shove. "Shut up. Listen, you're gonna like this." He shot a sidelong glance at Will. "Will's gonna take us glamping."

Kimmy's mouth fell open. "Wait, what? *You* are voluntarily going camping?" She frowned up at the ceiling. "Did the world end and I didn't notice?"

"Oh, ha-ha, you're hilarious." Koichi planted his hands on his hips. "He bet he could convert me to glamping. I bet he couldn't. It's that simple."

"I'll convert him," Will said before Kimmy could answer. "By the time I'm done, he'll be thanking me for introducing him to the best thing in the whole world."

Koichi gazed up at him with a clear challenge in his eyes. "We'll see."

"*You'll* see. I'm right." Will wiped off a dew of sweat from his upper lip. "So. Kimmy. D'you need any help next door?"

She beamed at him. "Such a gentleman. Thank you, sweetie, but I'm good. Everything's pretty much done. I came over to see if *you* needed anything."

There was still a good bit to do, but he hesitated to say so. Ever since leaving his family behind, he'd done his level best to stand on his own. The last thing he wanted to do now was take advantage of anyone and live down to his father's opinion of him.

You're a user, William. You won't be able to get along without your family. You need us. You need me. You need my money, you weak little piece of—

Koichi's voice jerked Will out of the unwelcome memory. "Hey, sis, would you mind too much going to get some dinner for us? I don't know about y'all, but I skipped lunch, and I'm *starving*." He clasped his hands together in supplication. "Please? We can all eat together, then finish up whatever work's left in here."

"Sure." She glanced from Koichi to Will. "Is Burger Barn okay with everybody? I could seriously go for a bacon double cheese right now."

Mmm. Cheeseburger. Will's stomach rumbled, reminding him that the oatmeal he'd had for breakfast was long gone. "That works for me."

"Me too." Koichi patted his pockets. "Kimmy, I'm buying for everybody, so take whatever money you need out of my wallet. I think I left it in the desk. You know where I usually keep it."

She nodded. "What d'you want?"

"Burger Barn Special with pepper jack and sweet potato fries. And an RC."

Will's mouth watered. "I'll have the same, only make my drink a sweet tea."

"Tea. Got it." Kimmy pulled her phone from the back pocket of her jeans, swiped it on, and tapped in the information. "Okay. Be back soon."

"Thank you," Will called to her as she pushed open the door.

She saluted with her phone, then strode out of sight.

A charged silence settled in. Will cleared his throat. "Okay. Well. Guess we should finish hanging that tent divider before Kimmy gets back with the food."

"I guess so." Koichi stepped close, his head tilted back, his hands in his pockets and his gaze locked onto Will's. "Gotta say, I'm glad I came over here. I think this could be the start of a beautiful friendship."

Will forced a laugh, in spite of the fist that closed over his heart. *Casablanca* was Anthony's favorite film. "I agree completely."

A strange expression came over Koichi's face—serious, watchful, inquisitive. As if he'd noticed Will's sudden sadness and wondered what it meant. Will held his breath. *Don't ask. Please don't ask.*

Either he was lucky or Koichi was psychic. He shook his head—shaking off his curiosity, Will thought—and smiled. "C'mon, Hood. Let's get busy."

By the time Kimmy got back with the burgers, Will and Koichi had the tent setup finished. The three of them sat cross-legged in the middle of the floor and ate, talking and laughing the whole time. Afterward, the twins insisted on hanging around to help Will finish setting up his various displays. He was grateful for more reasons than simply the work. Having them around drove away the pensive quiet, not to mention the loneliness that had dogged him ever since he left Houston.

No. Longer than that. Ever since Anthony had vanished more than two years ago. The rift his affair with Anthony had caused between him and his family had never healed. How could it? Growing up dyslexic, cripplingly shy, and homeschooled by a private tutor, he'd had no friends. All he'd had was his family. He'd thought they loved him unconditionally. They'd let him live at home while he earned his business degree from the University of Houston. Attending his dad's alma mater, then going to work for him—helping with payroll on the ranch—had gone a long way toward gaining him the approval and affection he'd always craved from his stern, distant father.

For a little while, at least. Then he'd fallen in love with a stable worker named Anthony Ruiz, and was forcibly reminded that his family's reputation mattered far more to them—especially to his father—than his happiness did.

Having people around who were there because they *liked* him was novel and fantastic. He didn't want it to end.

Kimmy stepped back from a portable table that she'd decorated with his best flatware and a lovely tin lantern with cutout stars. "I like it. What d'you think, Will?"

"It's gorgeous." He looked around his shop. Everything was in place, something that would've taken him at least a couple of days on his own. "It's *all* gorgeous. I never could've done this without you two. Thank you so, so much."

Smiling, Kimmy ran over, rose on her tiptoes, and kissed his cheek. "We were glad to do it, honey."

Koichi slapped him on the back. "Don't worry. We'll take our payment in tent-based servitude."

A whole series of decidedly impure images sashayed across Will's vision. He shoved them away, because, damn it, now was *not* the time. "I'm already looking forward to it."

"When are we going?" Kimmy peered up at him with an eager sparkle in her eyes. "Sorry, I don't mean to rush you or anything. It's just, I'm *super* excited. I've never been glamping before."

"Hmm." Will considered. "How about tomorrow night? The weather's supposed to be nice. And now that the shop's all set up, thanks to the two of you, I actually have the time to do it before the big opening on Friday." He glanced from Kimmy to her brother and back again. "What about it? Does that work for y'all?"

"Sounds good to me." Koichi raised his eyebrows at Kimmy. "What about it, sis?"

"Perfect. We don't open 'til Friday either." She squealed, grabbed Will's hands, and bounced on her toes. "Yay! This is gonna be so much fun!"

He laughed. "I'm going to make sure y'all have the time of your lives."

Koichi *hmph*ed, but a smile curled his lips and crinkled the corners of his eyes. "We'll see, my friend. We'll see." He grabbed his sister by the shoulders. "Let the man go, Kimmy. We need to lock up and get going. You promised Mama you'd stop by before you went home, remember?"

"Oh shit, I did, didn't I?" She dropped Will's hands and let her head fall backward with a heartfelt groan. "Okay, well, no point in putting it off. Will, gimme your phone, I'll put my number in. You can call me in the morning and tell me what time we need to be here."

"Okay." He fished his phone out of his pocket and handed it to her, and took hers when she shoved it at him. He thumbed on her phone, found the contacts, and started entering his information. "When should I call you?"

"Anytime. I'm usually up by six." She finished typing and glanced at Koichi, who was watching the two of them with transparent amusement. "I'll call Chichi later. He never gets up 'til like nine."

Will snickered as they traded phones again. "'Chichi'? Seriously?"

Koichi aimed a fierce frown at him. "Hey, it's silly, but it's not *that* bad."

They didn't know. That made it even funnier. Will laughed out loud.

The twins exchanged a *what the fuck* look, which made Will laugh harder, in spite of how stupid he was starting to feel.

"Wait, time-out." Koichi stepped in front of Will and stared up at him with a stubborn determination that he found dead sexy. "Explain why that's so funny."

Will grinned. "'Chichi' is Mexican slang for . . ." He stopped, remembering that he'd literally just met the twins today. Would they be offended? They didn't seem like the type. Especially Kimmy. But you never could tell. "Uh. You know." He held his hands cupped in front of his chest. "Bosoms. Only the T word."

The twins gaped at him. He had about half a second to notice for the first time how much they really did look alike. Then Koichi shook his head and turned away with a resigned sigh while Kimmy busted out laughing.

"You realize," Koichi said, raising his voice over his sister's guffaws, "that she's going to use this against me."

Will scratched his head. "Um . . ."

"Titty McNab! Oh my God." Kimmy wiped tears from her face. "Yeah, this is now a thing. Get used to it."

Koichi glared. Will hunched his shoulders. "Sorry?"

The death glare eased into something softer. Warmer.

Koichi covered his face with both hands. "Christ almighty. The two of you are a pain in my ass." He dropped his hands. A smile was fighting its way through the irritation. "All right. This subject is dead. See you tomorrow, Will."

He nodded. "Looking forward to it."

Kimmy reached up to wrap her arms around his neck and hugged him. "Talk to you then, honey. Night."

"Good night. And thank you both for everything."

They left in a flurry of *good-nights* and *see-you-laters*. He waited until they were out of sight, then went into the office to fetch his toothbrush and soap.

A few minutes later, face washed and teeth brushed, he flipped off the lights and stood at the back door watching the sun set over Hunter's Bog. Ever since arriving here a couple of weeks ago, he'd loved the serene, disheveled beauty of the marsh. It called him to explore—to take a canoe, or tramp off on foot, and search out the secrets of the crooked creeks, the moss-hung trees, the beds of reeds that whistled in the wind like lonely spirits. In the orange light of the sinking sun, the trees became black statues springing from rivers of fire.

In all his life, Will had never seen anything more stunning, or more mysterious.

He wondered if there was enough dry land in there for a decent campsite. The wheels in his brain started turning because he'd been born and raised as a businessman, and that was part of who he was. There had to be plenty of clients who'd pay for a luxury camping expedition into the bog. Especially the more well-off clients. If there was one thing he knew for a fact about people with too much money, it was that they were always on the lookout for the next exciting thing to relieve the boredom of their lives. Swamp glamping wasn't exactly on a par with exploring the Amazon, but it was different enough to appeal to the rich and adventurous.

He was still standing there mentally developing the idea when a swift movement in the marsh caught his eye. Frowning, he pressed his forehead to the window and cupped his hands around his eyes. Maybe he'd just seen a bird, or a squirrel. Even a deer. Animals were everywhere out there.

He'd almost convinced himself he'd imagined it when it happened again—a shadow, gray in the deepening dusk, flitting quick as thought from tree to tree. It had no discernible form, even when he squinted to see better.

A hard chill ran up Will's spine. He ignored it, flung open the door, and marched across the parking lot to the edge of the swamp.

The mid-April evening was warm and humid. A sluggish breeze flowed from the west in tired fits and starts, bringing with it the wet, earthy smell of the marsh. The crickets and bullfrogs and night birds he'd grown used to were strangely silent.

Try as he might, he couldn't see the shadow anymore. But he couldn't shake the sense of something watching.

He stood barefoot in the overgrown grass at the edge of the parking lot, peering into the growing dark, until the neck-prickling feel of unfriendly eyes on him eased and the familiar sounds of a Southern night returned. Finally, when full dark had fallen and the streetlamp at the end of the parking lot came on, he turned and went back inside.

He washed his feet before entering the display tent. Keeping it clean was important, since it had to double as his makeshift living space and a selling point for his business.

Gotta find a damn place to live.

That would have to wait until he'd made some actual money on this venture. With a deep sigh, he turned on the battery-powered lamp he'd bought at a yard sale, stretched out on the lounge chair with his book, and settled in to read.

CHAPTER 3

The three of them set off from the Hunter's Bog Mall back parking lot in Will's super-upscale truck the next afternoon around two thirty. Koichi leaned sideways to let the wind from the open window ruffle his hair. It was a gorgeous day, warm but not too hot, sunny and scented with new greenery. A perfect day to relax under the trees and have a handsome man see to his every need.

Speaking of which . . .

He glanced past Kimmy in the middle of the big bench seat to Will, who was steering with one hand and resting the other on the edge of the window frame. "Where're we going, exactly?"

"The Styx River. There's a bunch of great spots along it to set up camp, but I have a particular one in mind." Will shot him a grin full of excitement. "I can't believe y'all have never gone camping there."

"Told you I don't like camping," Koichi muttered.

Kimmy bumped his shoulder with hers. "Ignore him, Will. Our grammy used to take us camping when we were kids, but she liked to go to Little River State Park, where there's bathrooms and stuff. She liked tent camping, but she didn't like *primitive* camping."

"Well, I promise what you're gonna get with me isn't primitive in the least." He turned on his blinker and made a left turn onto a narrow, bumpy side road shaded by a thick growth of pines. "We'll be about fifteen minutes on this road, maybe, then we'll turn off toward the river."

"Cool. I can't wait." Kimmy beamed at Koichi. "How about it, T? You excited?"

Jesus give me strength. Koichi rubbed the side of his head, where he imagined he could feel his angry-vein throbbing. "Please don't call me that."

She snorted. "You'd rather I said the word?"

"I'd rather you called me by my *name*, you utterly annoying person."

"What's 'T' for?" Will asked before Kimmy could snark back.

Koichi pressed his lips together. If Will didn't know, he wasn't about to clear it up.

Of course Kimmy wasn't going to let it go. "Remember last night? When you told us what 'chichi' meant?"

Koichi glanced sideways in time to watch the lightbulb switch on in Will's brain. He snickered. "Oh."

Shit. This might be a really long day.

Will cleared his throat. "So. Koichi. Kimmy said you like shrimp. And Creole food."

"I do, yeah." He twisted around to peer at Will's profile. "Why?"

"No reason." One muscular shoulder hitched upward in a gesture of exaggerated casualness. "We're having shrimp étouffée for dinner, is all."

Goddamn. Koichi's stomach growled at the thought. "Mister, if you're making hush puppies with that, you're my new favorite person."

"Not just any hush puppies. My special beer-batter hush puppies. I picked up a locally brewed IPA for the batter. That's the secret." Will's lips curved into a smirk that shouldn't have been sexy, but was. "Best damn thing you'll ever taste in your life."

Kimmy hooted with laughter. "Is that confidence, or arrogance, Mr. Hood?"

Koichi waved a dismissive hand. "I don't care what you call it, as long as I get some of that cornmeal and beer goodness."

"As much as you want."

Something in the low, soft sound of Will's voice made Koichi look at him harder. His gaze was fixed out the front window, his attention on maneuvering around the potholes in the road. But his cheeks flamed pink, and Koichi could see the rapid pulse jumping in his throat.

Good golly, Miss Molly. Is he flirting?

Koichi swallowed hard. He sort of wished Kimmy wasn't in between them.

On the other hand, maybe it was a good thing she was. Groping the driver was probably a bad idea.

Kimmy turned a keen look on him, then on Will. "Oookay. How about some music?" She switched on the satellite radio and fiddled with it until she found a station playing the weird hipster pop she liked. "So, Will. How'd you decide to use the Styx River for your camping area? Is that where you're gonna take your customers?"

He lit up like a thousand-watt bulb. "Oh, I totally am. It's the *perfect* place for glamping. There's all these little beaches along the whole length of the river, and so many of them come with nice spots under the trees where I can set up tents. Listen . . ."

For the next few minutes Koichi listened, smiling, while Will gushed about all the beautiful campsites he'd found. Koichi found it frankly astounding how much Will had gotten done in the two short weeks since he'd arrived in Alabama. Sure, he'd researched and gotten the ball rolling on camping permits before moving, but still. He'd only rented the shop a month ago, and he'd decided to move to Alabama not long before that.

"Why'd you leave Houston?" Kimmy asked when Will stopped talking for a while.

His shoulders tensed. "I've lived around there my whole life. I just wanted to go someplace new, that's all."

That wasn't the whole story. Koichi knew it in his bones. He studied Will's profile, blank and unrevealing in the dappled afternoon shade. *What's your story, Will?*

Kimmy, as usual, had no idea when to stop. "But why here? I mean, sure, we're getting more people moving in these days. But most people who move here have a reason. Like, family or something." She patted Will's knee. "C'mon, honey. You're among friends here. Tell."

Will sucked on his lower lip, clearly uncomfortable, and Koichi felt compelled to rescue him. "Good grief, sis, leave him alone, would you? He obviously doesn't want to talk about it."

She frowned at Koichi, then cast a more thoughtful glance at Will. "I don't mean to pry. I like to know all about people. But look, if you don't want to answer something, or I'm overstepping my bounds, just say so, okay? I won't get offended or anything."

Some of the tightness eased from Will's neck and shoulders. "The reason I came here is pretty personal, and I'm not really sure I can explain it to anyone else. Sorry."

"Don't be." Koichi met Will's vulnerable, questioning glance with a smile. "You don't owe us any explanations, Will. It's fine."

Will didn't answer, but Koichi felt relief coming off him like a wave of energy.

Violins and banjo swelled from the radio to replace the lack of conversation following the world's most awkward moment. Koichi was glad. Part of him wanted to tell Will he could talk to him about anything, anytime. But another, larger part held up its nonexistent hands in his brain and said, *Nope.*

Kimmy always told him he was too emotionally distant and that's why he couldn't keep a man. She was halfway right. He knew he kept himself at a distance. But so far, all his relationships—other than with her—had proven that guarding himself was a fabulous idea. Christ, he could still remember Tristan's mind games like they'd happened yesterday: prying his most secret thoughts from him, then using them against him at every opportunity. Demanding complete honesty and giving none in return.

If that was what it meant to be open with someone, then he'd had enough of it in that one relationship to last ten lifetimes.

"Here it is."

Will's voice startled Koichi out of his navel-gazing. He sat forward as much as the seat belt would allow and stared in wide-eyed curiosity at the tiny gap between the pines toward which Will was now steering his truck.

His big, shiny, thus-far-unscratched truck.

Koichi had a feeling the unscratched part wasn't going to last long.

Evidently Kimmy's mind was going in the same direction as his, because she hissed in an anxious breath through her teeth as the truck slid through the opening into a dim green tunnel of overhanging branches. "Will, this is *not* doing your paint job any good."

"Don't worry about that." He grinned, excited as a child. "Trucks are for getting into tough places, like this one. If you just want a toy you can keep looking pretty, get a Jag."

Koichi laughed. "I like how you think."

Kimmy pursed her lips and said nothing, which only made him laugh harder. She treated her own truck better than some people treated their children.

If Will noticed the mini-drama in the seat beside him, he didn't let on. He was hunched over the wheel, his face a study in concentration. Not that Koichi blamed him. Calling the muddy little track they were driving on a "road" was pretty damn generous.

After a few minutes of bumping along, Koichi was about to ask how much farther it was, when the trail dumped them out of the trees onto an irregular patch of thin, scrubby grass. About twenty yards away, across a wide strip of golden sand, the Styx River flowed swift and shallow over a shoal of stones. Pines and cypress, hung with swaying beards of Spanish moss, shaded the water a deep brown at the edges, while the sun turned it clear amber in the middle. As Koichi watched, a big blue dragonfly landed on a patch of purple wildflowers blooming in the grass, then took off, flying toward the treetops.

"Fuck me sideways," he whispered. "This place is goddamn gorgeous."

Kimmy patted his knee. "Very poetical, T."

"Yeah, bite me." He leaned sideways and kissed her forehead as Will parked the truck at the edge of the grass. "Will, I gotta hand it to you. This really is a beautiful spot."

Kimmy nodded. "Totally. How on Earth did you find it?"

"Did some online research first. Then I asked around." Will turned off the engine, pocketed the keys, and smirked at them. "I'm not telling *all* my secrets, though. Now, since I don't have my staff yet, y'all're gonna help me unload and set up."

"I thought I was gonna get the four-star treatment on this trip," Koichi complained as he opened the door and hopped down from the cab. "What gives?"

"Oh, brother of mine, you're such a diva." Taking his hand in both of hers, she peered up at him, serious as a tax audit. "If you can't handle it, I'm sure it's okay if you go lie down on the divan and have the servants fan you for a while."

Will snickered. Koichi yanked his hand away, fighting a smile. "Shut up. Geez."

A solid hand gripped his shoulder. He peered into Will's gorgeous brown eyes, doing his level best not to swoon, because *damn*, the man was too hot for his own good. Koichi grinned. "Hey, you."

Hey, you? Really? Smooth, Casanova. Christ almighty.

Will dropped his hand and stepped back with a shy, sweet smile that set off miniature earthquakes in Koichi's belly. "Don't worry. Once we get everything set up, I'll wait on you all you want."

Oh, the promises in that not-so-innocent phrase. Koichi locked his knees so they wouldn't buckle and gave Accidental Innuendo Man what he sincerely hoped was a sexy smolder and not a creepy leering laser stare. "Mister, you keep promising me shit like that, I'll set up whatever you tell me to."

Okay, that sounded really stupid. But Will didn't seem to care, judging by how his expression went from sweet to sinful. He leaned close, his voice dropping low. "That's a deal, my friend."

Koichi stood rooted in place while Will went to open the bed of the pickup. Christ, he was so fucking screwed.

Setting up camp turned out to be a lot more fun than Koichi remembered from those long-ago days with Kimmy and Grammy. Maybe because this place was so peaceful. No radios blaring football games and clashing music stations, no shrieking children, no beer-fueled horseshoes competitions. Nothing but the birds singing and the constant, soothing chatter of the river. And Kimmy's occasional girlish giggle, but he was used to that, so it didn't count.

Will's deeper, masculine laughter affected him more. Caught him hard in the gut when he least expected it. Which was a bit disconcerting, but hey, he was a big boy. He could deal.

Once they'd gotten the tents and cookstove put together, Will shooed Koichi and Kimmy off toward the lounge chairs he'd strategically placed beside the river. Koichi smiled when he saw the little round table, complete with an open bottle of wine and two glasses, between the chairs. "Looks like our host has thought of literally everything."

"I'll say." Kimmy settled into the left-hand chaise, picked up the bottle, and studied the label. "Would you look at that? Your favorite cabernet."

"I see that." Koichi sank into the other chair and stretched out his legs. Mmm. Comfy. "How'd he know what wine I like?"

"I might've mentioned it." She filled both glasses, then recorked the bottle and took a sip. "This is the life right here, T. I could get used to it."

"Me too. Although I'm reserving judgment on the whole sleeping in a tent business." Koichi lifted his glass. "Cheers, sis."

"Cheers."

They clinked glasses. Koichi sipped his wine, watched the water flow over the stones, and told himself turning around to see what Will was doing would be creepy and weird.

"Do you like the wine?"

Startled, Koichi swallowed badly, got cabernet in his windpipe, and started coughing. He set his glass back on the table so he wouldn't spill it.

"Oh shit." Will's worried face came into view, leaning over Koichi, one hand hovering above his chest as if unsure whether or not to touch. "Sorry."

"It's okay," Koichi wheezed when he caught his breath. "I'm fine. You just surprised me, is all. Didn't know you were there."

A very fetching blush stained Will's cheeks. "I didn't mean to sneak up on you."

"Not your fault. My mind was a million miles away." Koichi smiled. He couldn't help it. The man was just so damned adorable. "And the wine is perfect. My favorite, actually. Thank you."

The blush deepened. Will straightened up, studying the ground at his feet. "Kimmy told me what you liked."

"She's a good sister now and then." Koichi grinned, ignoring Kimmy's indignant *hey*. "Can't you sit down with us and have a glass?"

Will's eyes widened. "Oh. I don't know. I'm supposed to be working."

Kimmy dismissed that excuse with a loud raspberry. "Please, it's just Chichi and me. You don't have to be all professional with us."

"She's right." Koichi picked up the bottle and waggled it at Will. "C'mon. You know you want to."

Will gnawed on his bottom lip, his face a battleground between his businessman side and his hanging-out-with-friends side. God, that was cute. *Pick hanging out, Will. Please, please, please.*

Maybe Will was psychic, because he grinned and nodded as if he'd heard Koichi's silent begging. "Okay, y'all talked me into it. Let me go grab another chair."

"No need." Kimmy jumped up, her glass in hand. "Take mine. I was just thinking I'd go for a walk along the river. I mean, it's so pretty, you know, and I've never been here before."

"Oh." Will edged toward her abandoned chair, eyes narrowed. "I have another chair. You don't need to get up."

"I know. Seriously, I want to check out that path along the river." She pointed toward a narrow trail through the trees. "Where's your wineglasses, hon? I'll get you one." She trotted off toward the truck before Will could go himself.

He watched her with a frown. "That basket there next to the stove. Um, thanks." Shaking his head, he settled into Kimmy's abandoned chair with the air of a man doing something illicit. "Damn."

That one word held all the mingled admiration and frustration Koichi had felt for his sister all his life. He chuckled. "I feel you, man."

Kimmy cleared her throat behind them, making him jump. She cast him an amused look as she filled the glass she'd brought over and handed it to Will. "There you go. You boys behave yourselves. I'll be back after a while."

"Thank you," Will called after her. "Enjoy your walk."

"Watch out for snakes!" Koichi called.

She glared over her shoulder. He waved at her.

Will shook his head as Kimmy tromped off through the woods, the pine straw crackling beneath her feet. "I swear, you two are hilarious."

"Glad we could entertain you." Koichi shifted in his seat so he could see Will better, picked up his glass, and took a healthy swallow of the luscious, full-bodied cabernet. "You know what, I don't even care about the tent. I'm kicking back in a gorgeous private spot, sharing my favorite wine with a handsome man who also happens to be extremely kind and thoughtful. I am one lucky bastard."

The blush that had faded from Will's face returned, staining his cheeks pink. He smiled his sweet, shy smile, knotting the noose a little tighter around Koichi's heart. Not that he minded. "I'm glad you're having fun. That's all I wanted."

Goddamn. Heart thumping, Koichi reached across the table with his free hand to touch Will's arm. "I am. We both are."

"Good." Will's eyes cut away. Back to Koichi. Away again. Nervous, obviously. "Y'all are my test cases, I guess. I mean, I brought you out here 'cause I wanted to thank you for everything you did to help me. But, yeah. I guess I'm kind of testing out my business model on you. Sorry."

Koichi dismissed the *sorry* thing with a vigorous shake of his head. "Nope. None of that. It's a victimless crime. And you are *so* gonna kill it at this whole glamping thing. You're a wonderful host. You make your customers feel like they're the most important people in the world. And this place?" He gestured with his wineglass—gently, so he wouldn't spill. "I mean, come on. Even the most die-hard fan of city living is gonna love it. Especially since you're pampering them with comfy beds and awesome home cooking." He leaned sideways, aiming his Very Serious Stare at Will. "I ought to know."

That got him a laugh. "Okay. Thanks for that."

They sat there for a while, enjoying the wine and the river view without speaking. The silence was comfortable, to Koichi's surprise. He usually felt the need to correct a lack of conversation, but with Will, mutual quiet didn't seem like a problem.

That ought not to scare him, but it did.

Oh well. Kimmy had always said he was afraid of commitment.

"Koichi?"

He blinked himself out of his thoughts, trying to pretend his mind hadn't wandered into his morose why-aren't-I-in-a-relationship space. "Hmm? Yeah?"

Will's smile was gentle. Tender, even. "You okay?"

"Oh, yeah. Just thinking." He gulped wine. Good Lord, Will's gaze could skewer a mastodon. But the shadow in those deep-brown eyes said something specific was on his mind. Something other than Koichi's mental well-being. "What's up?"

Will shrugged. "Nothing much. I just had an idea, and I sort of wanted your opinion about it."

Okay, that was intriguing. "Well, I'm always happy to opine about things. What is it?"

"Hunter's Bog." Will's lips tilted into a dreamy smile. A faraway look softened his features. "It's pretty incredible. I was thinking I could take clients out there, but I don't really know that much about it." His gaze sharpened again, focusing on Koichi's face. "You've lived in this area for a long time. Do you think camping in the bog is doable?"

Koichi wanted to say no, on general principle. The damn place was a hotbed of bugs, mud, and general grossness. But that was *his* opinion. He had to be fair, for Will's sake.

"Most of it is too wet and marshy," he said. "But there's islands in the interior that're big enough and dry enough to camp on. You can get maps and stuff from the state Department of the Interior website."

Will nodded, his expression thoughtful. "That sounds perfect. I can keep the groups small for the bog trips."

"Definitely." Fascinated, Koichi watched Will's face as the wheels turned in his mind. "You know Hunter's Bog's haunted, right?"

Will pinned Koichi with a sharp stare. "What do you mean, haunted?"

"You know. Haunted. With the ghosts of hunters that've disappeared there. Thus the name." Koichi frowned at the intense look in Will's eyes. Sure, it was an interesting local legend, but not *that* interesting. "Hey, that's just a story. You don't really *believe* it, do you?"

For a couple of seconds, Will didn't answer. He turned to peer out over the river, his forehead furrowed. "No, of course not. Just wondering how I could use it for the glamping expeditions. Ghost stories at night, maybe?"

Koichi's gut told him that wasn't what Will was thinking at all. But it wasn't his place to say so. "Sounds like fun to me."

Will didn't answer. Koichi glanced at him. He held his glass against his chin, as if unsure whether he wanted to drink or not. His lower lip was caught between his teeth, and his gaze was focused inward.

Curiosity ate at Koichi's insides. What was going on behind that handsome face? Had Will seen one of the famous spirits of Hunter's Bog? But why would that bother him so much that he'd zoned out in the middle of the conversation? It didn't make any sense.

Oh well. The day wasn't over yet. The way Koichi figured it, he had plenty of time to work on Will and get the information out of him.

Settling deeper into the comfy lounge chair, Koichi sipped his wine and started plotting his approach.

CHAPTER 4

Opening day blew away all Will's expectations. By the time he locked up over an hour after the official closing time, his stock was severely depleted and he'd been going for more than twelve hours without a break, but he was too excited to care.

He wasn't the only one, judging by the mood at the owners' party that night in the back parking lot.

"I've already ordered more tents, lanterns, sleeping bags, and cookstoves. And I've booked several Styx River trips too." He thumbed the condensation from the beer bottle in his hand—his third, not that he was counting—and grinned at Koichi. "Who knew the folks around here were so into glamping?"

Koichi gave him an *Are you serious right now?* look. "You, I hope. Otherwise, this was a pretty whacko business model." He sipped from his water bottle, watching Will with amusement in his eyes. "I'm glad it was a good day."

"Thanks. It really was." Will glanced around at the group of shop owners and employees milling around the parking lot, drinking beer and sodas, munching chips, and talking over the satellite radio music blasting through Eastern Shore Archery's screen door. "How did you and Kimmy do?"

Koichi's face lit up with a smile that did interesting things to Will's insides. "Fantastic. A bunch of our regulars from the old shop came over, which was cool. And we sold *lots* of soaps and candles to people just passing through."

"That's wonderful. I'm glad."

Kimmy's laughter rang out behind him. He turned, caught her gaze, and shared a smile with her. She practically glowed with happiness. He watched her for a moment, wishing he could absorb some of her joy. Not that he was *un*happy, exactly. But for the last two years, he'd felt like everything good in his life was tainted by the question mark Anthony had left behind when he vanished.

Beyond Kimmy and the knot of owners chatting over the snack table, out in the bog, something moved. Frowning, Will peered deeper into the shadows, but whatever it was, he couldn't see it anymore.

Probably a deer or something. He turned his back to the darkness reluctantly, to find Koichi staring into the swamp with intense concentration. Will's scalp prickled. "Koichi? What is it?"

"I don't know. I thought I saw . . ." His forehead furrowed. "I thought something moved out in the bog."

Will glanced over his shoulder. Kimmy was deep in conversation with a few other owners. None of them seemed to have noticed anything out of the ordinary. He turned back to Koichi. "I saw something too. Couldn't tell what it was, though. Just a movement."

"Huh." Koichi tilted his head sideways, lips pursing. He tapped a fingertip on his water bottle. The thin plastic crackled. "It was probably just an animal. An owl, maybe."

He sounded doubtful. Will didn't blame him. Whatever they'd seen, it was unnaturally stealthy and silent.

The group around the table all laughed at once, almost drowning out the music. The very loud music. Okay, so possibly any sounds made by an animal moving through the bog could've been swallowed up by the party noise.

He couldn't help feeling a little disappointed.

Which Koichi totally picked up on, judging by his grin. "What's the matter, Will? You wishing the haunted bog stories were true?"

He shrugged, cheeks heating. "Maybe a little bit."

"It's okay, man. I get it. It's fun to think the place is crawling with ghosts, even if it's really not." Koichi stuck his free hand in the front pocket of his pants—sturdy black denim that clung gorgeously to his wiry body—leaned in a bit, and lowered his voice. "Kimmy says my house is haunted."

Will raised his eyebrows. "Seriously?"

"Yep. It's Grammy and Grampa McNab's old place. It was built in the late 1800s." Koichi grinned. "Lots of time to collect ghosts, right?"

Ghosts. Spirits of the dead and the vanished.

Anthony's face rose in Will's mind. It was Anthony as he'd last seen him, grim and gray-faced beneath his soft brown skin, his dark eyes red-rimmed and sad, swearing he was fine in spite of all the evidence to the contrary.

The next day, he hadn't answered Will's calls. Will had never seen or heard from him again. And after all this time, after two years of silence, the fact that Anthony had spent their last night together pretending nothing was wrong still hurt.

"Will? Did you hear me?"

Shit. Why did he let himself zone out like that?

He forced a smile. "Sorry. What'd you say?"

"I said, my grandparents found a bunch of old jewelry and other things in the attic of the house after they bought it. Kimmy put some of it out in our old shop for decoration." Koichi stepped closer, peering up at Will with worry in his eyes. "Are you okay?"

"Oh, yeah. I'm fine." Will widened his fake smile until his cheeks hurt. "I was just thinking about how great today was."

The concern in Koichi's face morphed into suspicion. "No, you weren't."

Okay, that was blunt. Will drank from his beer to cover his surprise. "You don't know what I'm thinking."

"Maybe not *exactly*. But if you were thinking about what an awesome day you had, you wouldn't've looked like somebody strangled your puppy." Koichi pointed at Will with his water-bottle hand. "Something's bothering you. You don't have to tell me what it is. But don't pretend nothing's wrong when something obviously is."

Coming hot on the heels of his own thoughts about Anthony, the words felt like a kick in the chest. Maybe the universe was trying to tell him something.

"I came here to find someone." The confession escaped before he could consider whether or not it was a good idea. *Go on and get it off your chest*, said the three beers. *You'll feel better.* "A man I loved, once. I thought he loved me too, but . . ."

Koichi gulped the last of his water and crushed the bottle, watching Will with a blank, cautious expression. "But what?"

Yeah, Will? What? He shook his head. "I haven't seen him or heard from him in two years. But I know he's alive. I know he's in this area, somewhere. If he ever really cared about me, why didn't he contact me? In two whole years, why hasn't he ever tried to contact me?"

The bitterness in his voice shocked him. He thought he'd gotten past that by now.

Evidently not.

Koichi looked away, watching whatever was going on behind Will's left shoulder. "What's his name?"

"Anthony Ruiz." Will shifted from foot to foot, feeling more uncomfortable by the second. He hadn't hidden his sexuality from Koichi, but he hadn't announced it either. Until now. And he realized, too late, that he had no idea how his newfound friend would feel about it. "Look, Koichi—"

"I could help you find him."

Okay, that was unexpected. Will gaped. "Huh?"

Koichi shrugged, obviously trying for nonchalance but failing miserably. "I was born and raised in this area. Between Kimmy and me, we know practically everyone around here." He scuffed the toe of one sneaker against the pavement, eyes downcast. "If Anthony's in the Duchene area, somebody's bound to have seen him, right? So, yeah. I can help."

Will slapped a mosquito off his neck and tried to weigh Koichi's level of sincerity. He couldn't see beyond the bland mask Koichi had plastered over his usually expressive features. "Um. All right. I'd really appreciate that. If you're sure you want to do it. You don't have to."

Koichi rolled his eyes. "I wouldn't've offered to help if I didn't want to. C'mon, don't be stupid. Let me help you."

His tone was gentler than his words. Which did nothing to rid Will of the awkwardness dragging at him like Marley's chains. It made no sense, but there it was.

Still, he'd come here looking for Anthony. And Koichi might be the key to finding him. So . . .

"Okay." Will laughed. "You're right. I'm being stupid, and you're being amazing, as usual." Moved to action by the smile curving Koichi's mouth, he wrapped both arms around Koichi and pulled him into a hard embrace. "Thank you. You don't know . . ." His throat closed up, and his eyes stung. In all the time Anthony had been missing, no one else had cared. Not his family, not his so-called friends. He hadn't realized until now how lonely his grief had been.

Koichi's arms went around Will, hands rubbing circles on his back. "Hey, what're friends for, right?" He patted Will's shoulder and drew back, concern stamped all over his face. "Let's sit down. You can tell me all about Anthony. It'll make you feel better."

He was right. Will nodded. "Yeah. Okay."

Koichi led the way to the strip of grass between Will's back door and his own. They sat side by side, far enough from the festivities to talk comfortably but close enough to feel like they hadn't actually gone off alone.

"So." Koichi looped his arms around his knees, his attention focused on the shadows out in the bog. "How did you and Anthony meet?"

"The foreman on my family's ranch hired him to groom the horses." Will smiled, remembering the morning he'd walked into the barn to saddle his mare, Josephine, and found the shirtless Latino man singing "Let Me Call You Sweetheart" to her while he brushed her down. "It was lust at first sight, for me anyway. He wouldn't give me the time of day at first."

"But you wore him down?"

"Yep."

Koichi let out a low laugh. "I can totally see that."

Will cast him a sidelong glance. He turned to meet Will's gaze, green eyes bright with curiosity, and Will looked away. "He was afraid he'd get fired if we started seeing each other and my dad found out. But we had so much in common. We both loved camping, and being outdoors. We both loved cooking. He knew all about wilderness survival, and he taught me everything he knew." He smiled, remembering. "He never would tell me how he'd learned. He said he wanted to keep a little bit of mystery."

Koichi laughed, a soft noise barely audible over the party. "He sounds like a fascinating guy."

"He was, yeah." Will watched his fellow shop owners eating, drinking, and mingling across the parking lot. "We both had dyslexia.

He was the only other person I'd ever met at the time who'd had to cope with that growing up. Just talking about it with him made me feel less alone."

"I can imagine." Koichi laid a hand on Will's knee. "It must've been hard dealing with that."

"Sometimes." In fact, it had been incredibly difficult. He still had trouble. But it wasn't something he liked to dwell on, or talk about. "But he *got* that, you know? I mean, we had different backgrounds. I'd grown up rich; he'd grown up middle class. But we understood each other. My horse even liked him."

A half smile tilted one corner of Koichi's mouth. "I don't know shit about horses, but I'm thinking that must count for a lot."

"You're thinking correctly."

Koichi studied him as if he'd like to drill inside his head. "What happened?"

Will knew what he was asking. Taking a deep breath, he shut his eyes and went back in time. "We were together for a year and a half. It was . . . incredible. I was homeschooled and isolated as a kid. I commuted to college, then stayed on the ranch for my first job. Anthony was the first person I ever was really close to. Then . . ." His throat went tight. *Breathe, Will. Just breathe.* He opened his eyes, watching the fireflies blink in the bog. "One day, he was just gone. He didn't say where. Didn't tell me he was going. He just vanished."

He felt Koichi's stare burning into the side of his skull. "Was it your dad?"

The familiar anger and betrayal closed like a fist around his heart. "He wouldn't admit it. But why else would Anthony have left like that, without a word to me? We loved each other, Koichi. He wouldn't have done that unless someone had threatened him. And who would've done that except my father?"

The fact that the old man had denied it right up until Will had stormed out of his study for the last time had never stopped hurting. *I fired him because the help does not mix with the house. But I did not make him leave town. That was his own doing. Not that I blame him.*

God, the sneer on his father's face that day had cut deeper than it ever had before. They hadn't spoken since that morning. His father hadn't called, or written, or otherwise tried to contact him. Not during the year and a half he'd lived on his own in Houston, and not since he'd moved to Alabama. Neither had anyone else in his family, probably because they were afraid of what his dad would say. He hadn't tried to speak to any of them either, and the pain of their silence was still raw.

Koichi squeezed Will's knee. "I've had some rotten boyfriends before. But at least I've always had my family on my side. I'm sorry." He peered at Will with the sort of understanding he'd craved all his life. "I know you need some closure from this guy. I hope we can find him."

Will couldn't speak past the lump in his throat, but a subconscious weight lifted from his heart and didn't return.

The party started to wind down after another hour or so. By that time, Will had a four-beer buzz going and was feeling pretty damn good.

Kimmy hooked her arm through his as the two of them followed Koichi to Kimmy's truck. "Hey, why don't I give you a lift home?"

He shook his head. "Naw, it's okay."

Koichi turned around and walked backward, frowning. "Sorry, but you drank too much to get behind the wheel. So either one of us is driving you home, or you're sleeping in your shop."

Will snickered. The twins stared at him like he'd lost his mind. Of course, they didn't know why that was funny, so . . .

"I *am* sleeping at the shop." He laughed harder at the identical *What the fuck?* looks that got him. Tomorrow he was going to be embarrassed about this, but right now, he was sort of enjoying it. "I haven't found a place to live yet. So I'm staying in the tent in my shop."

Kimmy's eyes widened. "Oh my *God.*" She smacked his arm. "Why didn't you say something before? You can come stay with me or Koichi until you find a place. You *idiot.*" She hit him again, harder this time.

"Ow." He rubbed the spot where her hand had left a stinging mark. "Damn. For a little thing, you sure do hit hard."

Koichi grinned. "You don't know the half of it. Try growing up with her."

"I won't dignify that with a response." She cast her brother a swift, murderous look, then peered up at Will with green eyes full of concern. "Seriously, Will, you know you're welcome to stay with either of us." Her slender fingers tightened on his arm. "Why don't you get your stuff and come on home with me? My apartment has a second bedroom. It's not very big, but it's comfortable. You can stay as long as you need to."

He hesitated. It was a truly kind offer, and he didn't want her to think he didn't appreciate it, because he did. But the whole thing felt strange and uncomfortable. Growing up, he'd always had his own suite of rooms, away from his parents, siblings, aunts, uncles, grandparents, and various cousins who all shared the sprawling mansion. The only person he'd ever felt right sharing his personal space with was Anthony. And look how *that* had turned out.

"You can stay with me if that's more comfortable for you," Koichi said while Will was still fumbling for an answer that didn't sound horrifically snooty. "There's plenty of room in my house." He flashed an odd, tight smile. "You don't ever have to see me unless you want to."

"Um." Having no idea what exactly that meant or how to respond, Will rubbed the back of his neck and glanced around him at the darkened shop doors, the bog, the moths fluttering around the parking lot lights—anywhere but Koichi.

Kimmy dropped Will's arm, went to her brother, and took his hands. "You don't have to, T."

Her voice was soft, barely audible above the night noises from the bog, but Will heard anyway. He frowned. What was that all about? Crap, he hoped Koichi didn't think he was obligated to offer Will a place to sleep.

Koichi said something Will couldn't hear, then dug his keys out of his pocket and clicked the fob. The taillights on his car flashed. He went around to the driver's side, opened the door, and peered at Will in the yellowish interior light. "The offer stands, Will. And I mean it, okay? You have my number. Call me if you change your mind." He slid behind the wheel and shut the door.

Will didn't point out that he'd never actually responded to Koichi's offer. His answer would've been the same as to Kimmy: no.

Too close, too intimate. Especially with Koichi, because of the attraction Will couldn't help. A tent in a shop wasn't an ideal place to live, but it gave him the space and privacy he needed.

Kimmy cast him a sidelong glance as the two of them strolled toward the back door of his shop. "You sure you're gonna be okay here?"

"Yeah, I'll be fine. It's really not bad." He glanced toward the end of the parking lot where Koichi's car had rounded the edge of the mall into the front. He wondered what Koichi was thinking right now. If he was glad Will hadn't come with him, or wished he had.

Outside the door to Will's shop, Kimmy stopped, turned to face him, and grasped both his hands in hers. "You need your space. I totally get that. But look, if you change your mind, give me a call, okay? Or Koichi. He can be kind of distant and weird sometimes, but I've known him all my life, and I can tell right now that he would not hesitate to take you into his home if you asked. Guaranteed. So promise me you'll call one of us if you decide you want someplace else to stay, all right?"

A rush of affection surged through him, warming him to his toes. "I promise." Smiling, he bent to kiss her cheek. "Thank you, Kimmy. For everything."

"My pleasure." She squeezed his fingers hard, then let go. "I'll see you tomorrow. Sweet dreams."

"You too."

He waited outside until she climbed into her truck and drove off, then unlocked the shop door and went inside. The place was dark and silent.

For a moment, he wished he'd gone with Kimmy, or Koichi. Someplace bright and warm, where he didn't have to be alone. Then old insecurities poked their heads out of the soil, reminding him that when he was alone, he didn't have to explain anything. He didn't have to justify his thoughts, his feelings, or what he did. Alone was easier.

Better? Maybe. Maybe not. But definitely easier.

The day's good mood gone, he shoved his hands in his pockets and slouched toward his lonely tent.

Saturday morning arrived before Will was ready for it. Yawning, he hauled himself out of the camp cot, straightened the covers, and dragged himself into the bathroom to wash up and dress.

You could've had a shower instead of a spit-bath in the sink. And you could've slept in a real bed. Bet you still could if you ask nicely.

He sighed. His inner voice had always loved its creature comforts.

Good thing he'd trained himself to resist that too-sensible whisper. Honestly, just being around Koichi turned him into a tongue-tied moron. That being the case, living with the man seemed like a terrible idea.

Staying with Kimmy might be fun. But she was relentless and fearless, and he wasn't sure he was ready to open up his whole life to someone he barely knew.

In the mirror, his hollow-eyed reflection smiled a twisted, bitter smile. "You're pathetic, Will. Sad and pathetic."

God, that was disgusting. He turned away from his own sad eyes and marched to the storeroom to pick out the day's wardrobe from the shelf he'd designated as his closet.

He had to laugh at himself. A grown man, not only living in a shop, but in a *tent* in a shop? Yep. Pathetic.

After he'd gotten the shop all set for the day's opening, he walked to Bog Brew, the coffee shop a couple of doors down, for some breakfast. He spent a few minutes talking to the morning manager—an outgoing young woman with pink hair and an infectious laugh—then headed over to McNab's carrying three fair-trade coffees and three egg, bacon, and Swiss bagels.

"I brought breakfast," he announced when Kimmy let him in. "I didn't know if y'all had eaten yet or not, but you can always save it for later if you don't want it right now."

"I want it." Koichi claimed his share of food and caffeine with a grin. "You're awesome, Will. Thank you."

Predictably, his cheeks heated. "No problem. It's literally the least I can do after all you've both done for me."

Kimmy dismissed that idea with a snort-and-eye-roll combination. "What, letting you take us glamping? Yeah, that was a *huge* sacrifice." She fished a bagel sandwich out of the bag and started unwrapping it. "Face it, Mr. Hood: you're just a nice guy."

Will blushed harder. "Speaking of glamping, I'd like to do a test run out in the bog before I take clients out there. Get a feel for what the conditions are like, and what all I'd need. Do either of you want to come with me? Don't feel like you *have* to. I can do it on my own. But you're welcome to come, if you want."

He said nothing about how much he actually needed the help. *Desperation is so unattractive, hon*, said his mother's image in his mind.

To his surprise, Koichi was the one who spoke up. "I'll go."

Kimmy's eyebrows rose. "Wow. You realize this means he's converted you and you now owe him money."

"No, he doesn't," Will said before Koichi's scowl could turn into an argument with his sister. "That bet wasn't serious. I'm just happy to have your help, Koichi. Thank you."

Those pretty lips curved into a smile that made Will weak in the knees. "My pleasure. Especially if you make those awesome hush puppies again. Not that I'm hinting or anything."

"Hey, you're braving the bog for me." Will pulled a piece of bacon out of his sandwich and nibbled one end. "I'll make you anything you want."

All the playfulness vanished from Koichi's face. His gaze turned hot and knowing, and Will's mouth went dry.

A knock on the glass door startled him. He turned, heart thudding hard. Kimmy was already opening the door to let in a cadaverously thin middle-aged man in a suit a couple of sizes too big for him. "Hi, Detective Beauchamp. How're you doing?"

"Just fine, Ms. McNab." The detective pushed his sunglasses to the top of his head and mopped sweat from his brow. He darted a sharp, assessing look at Will. "I don't believe we've met, Mr. . . ."

"Will Hood." Will crossed the room to shake the man's hand. "I own the shop next door."

"I see. Nice to meet you." Beauchamp shook only as long as propriety demanded, then dropped Will's hand as if it might bite him. "I'm sorry, Mr. Hood, but I need to discuss something private with the McNabs. If you'll excuse us?"

"Oh. Yeah, of course." Will gathered his coffee and bagel and cast an apologetic glance at the twins. "Sorry. I'll just head on back over to my place. Koichi, we'll work out details of the camping trip later."

Koichi touched his arm as he passed, sending a shock up his arm. He smiled, Koichi smiled back, and his chest tightened.

He walked back to his shop on rubbery legs. Good God, what in the hell was he getting himself into?

Koichi watched Will go and wished he'd asked him to stay. Whatever Detective Beauchamp was here for, it couldn't be anything they'd be happy to hear. He'd been part of the fire case from the beginning, because that was the nature of the beast. But so far they hadn't seen much of him, and never when there was *good* news.

Maybe Will couldn't actually help, but his presence felt strong and comforting.

Kimmy took his hand, squeezing hard. "Okay, Detective. What do you have to tell us?"

For a few seconds, he stood there cracking his knuckles and not speaking, which made Koichi nervous. He clung to his sister's hand and reminded himself that giving the cops "sass" (as Grammy called it) was a bad idea.

Finally, Beauchamp sighed. "Well, I guess there's no way to say it but to just say it. So here it is. It looks like the fire at your old shop was started by a candle burning in the front room. It was apparently knocked over, and the flame caught on the fabric covering the front of the checkout desk."

Oh Christ. Koichi shut his eyes. The knowledge felt like a physical weight dragging him to the ground.

Naturally, Kimmy wasn't having any of his angst. She dropped his hand, set down her coffee, grabbed his shoulders, and shook him until he opened his eyes to meet her hard, determined stare. "Stop it, Koichi. It wasn't your fault, okay?"

"But I left the candle burning." His voice was a whisper—shaking, defeated. He hated it. "I don't remember, but I must have. I was the only one there."

"And that could have happened to any of us." She shook him again. "We sell candles, sweetie. We all burned them from time to time. *All* of us. It could have been me, or Mom, or Dad, or Grammy. Anybody. You hear? It wasn't. Your. Fault."

Each word was punctuated with another shake. He grabbed her wrists. "Sis, I love you, but you're making me dizzy."

Detective Beauchamp cleared his throat. "There's one other thing."

Hope and dread churned in Koichi's stomach, making him wish he hadn't eaten any of that bagel sandwich yet. He hunched his shoulders and forced himself to look at the detective instead of hiding behind his sister. "What?"

"We found traces of accelerant at the scene." Beauchamp pinned him with a narrow-eyed stare. "We might be looking at arson."

CHAPTER 5

Arson. An ugly word for an ugly act. The weight of Koichi's guilt eased, but the gut-punched feeling that replaced it wasn't any better.

"Hang on." Kimmy planted one hand on her hip and pointed at the detective with the other. "You're not trying to say either of us burned down our shop, are you?"

Better not be, said her fierce frown and snapping eyes. For his own part, Koichi couldn't get a single word out past his astonishment. He'd been beating himself up over his carelessness and stupidity all this time. Being accused of arson had never even crossed his mind.

Detective Beauchamp shook his head, one hand held palm-out toward them. "No, neither of you are under suspicion at this time. That said, since it was your place and you stood to benefit from the insurance money—"

Kimmy snorted. "Oh, please."

"We didn't even get enough to rebuild." Anger prickled Koichi's neck and scalp. "That's why we're out here instead of back in Duchene."

Beauchamp pinched the bridge of his nose. "As I was saying. Because you two owned the building and were the insurance beneficiaries—regardless of the amount—we'll need to talk to you both. Just ask a few questions, that's all. Particularly you, Mr. McNab, since you were the one actually in the building at the time."

Dread crept into Koichi's limbs, leaving him weak and shaky. "I didn't burn down my shop. Hell, I barely got out alive myself."

The other man drew a deep breath and blew it out. He might as well have had *impatient* carved into his forehead. "Once again, you are *not* under suspicion. Okay? But you have to understand that we need to question you, and your sister. We need to eliminate you both as suspects for certain. Also, since you were physically present in the shop when it caught fire, you may have seen or heard something that will help us figure out what happened. Sometimes people notice things that they don't even realize are important."

He still felt like a suspect. But he knew he hadn't done anything—well, not on purpose—so he had nothing to worry about. Right?

Maybe. But it didn't stop him from worrying.

Kimmy touched his shoulder. "It'll be fine, T. Let's just go on and get it over with."

She was right. He sighed. "All right. But I'm bringing my breakfast with me."

The detective smiled. "Fine by me. Y'all know where the police station is, right?"

Kimmy nodded. "We'll meet you there."

"Great. See you in a few minutes." Beauchamp slid his shades back into place, turned, and strode outside.

Kimmy followed and locked the door behind him. "Well. Guess we're opening late today."

"Yeah. I didn't know these guys even did interrogation stuff on the weekend." Koichi gathered his coffee and the rest of his sandwich—growing cold now—and headed for the back door with his sister at his heels. "This had better worth the lost business."

"I'm not holding my breath." She glanced up at him with a wry smile. "But you never know, right? Gotta stay positive."

A familiar affection swelled inside him. He and his twin got on each other's nerves a lot, but they'd always had one another's backs. And he *needed* her upbeat outlook on life.

He bumped her arm with his. "I'll drive."

They returned in a considerably worse mood than when they'd left. Which for Koichi wasn't a stretch, to be honest. But it took a lot to dampen Kimmy's spirits.

Like answering the same questions for two hours straight, apparently.

She threw her purse onto the floor and plopped into the chair so hard it squealed in protest. "Good grief. If they actually ever get their thumbs out of their asses long enough to find whoever *did* burn down our place, I hope they give him half the grilling they just gave us."

"Amen to that." Koichi perched on the edge of the desk and rubbed at the ache throbbing in his temple. "Do we have any ibuprofen in the desk? I've got a wicked headache."

"I think so. Hang on." She bent to dig through the big bottom drawer where they kept various odds and ends.

A knock rattled the screen door leading to the rear parking lot. "Hello? Y'all in there?"

Will. Koichi's heart did the funny little jump it tended to do when Will was around. "In the office," he called. "C'mon in."

The screen door creaked open and banged shut. Will walked into the office, his dark brows pulled together in concern. "Hey. I saw you come back. Are you guys all right?"

"Yeah," Koichi answered at the same time as Kimmy said, "No."

Will cast an understandably cautious look between them. "Okay. What happened?"

"The cops gave us the third degree." Kimmy straightened up and handed Koichi the little bottle of painkillers. "Do all detectives and policemen have problems with short-term memory loss, or is it just the ones in Duchene?"

Koichi laughed at Will's confused expression. "They questioned us for, like, two hours, and it was pretty much the same questions over and over again. It was pretty irritating."

"I can imagine." Will watched Koichi open the ibuprofen bottle and shake two pills into his palm. "You okay?"

He nodded. "Just a headache. They grilled us pretty hard. Plus they found out we'd been robbed, so that was kind of bad news."

Will's eyes saucered. "Oh my God. When did that happen?"

Koichi glanced at Kimmy, who shrugged as if to say, *your call.* He sighed. "Go on and explain it, sis."

She summarized the conversation they'd had earlier at the shop with Detective Beauchamp while Koichi went to the minifridge in the corner, dug out a bottled water, and swallowed the pills.

"I had given the cops a list of all the stuff in our shop at the time of the fire," Kimmy was saying when he went back to the desk. "Our sales inventory, the stuff in the office, the displays, everything. The list I gave the insurance company, basically. It was just procedure, you know? Nobody expected anything to come of it. But today, the detective tells us that the jewelry from our display behind the checkout counter was missing."

Will frowned. "It couldn't've been destroyed in the fire?"

"Well, that's what we thought." Koichi picked at the label on the water bottle, turning over everything he'd learned in his head yet again. "But Beauchamp said the fire chief told him that there ought to have been *something* left, even if it was just bits of melted metal."

"They're not *positive* we were robbed," Kimmy added. "But they think it's the most likely scenario."

Koichi nodded. "Especially since they found accelerant at the scene."

"Hmm." Will rubbed his chin, his gaze turned inward. "I don't like this at all. Whoever did that is still out there. What if they try to rob you again?"

"I've been thinking about that," Kimmy said, reflecting Koichi's own thoughts. "And you're right. The perp is still out there."

Koichi snickered. "The perp?"

She shot him a murderous glare. "Shut up, Titty." Ignoring his scowl and Will's poorly stifled laugh, she clasped her hands together on the desk and put on her serious look. "Anyway, as I was saying. The *perp*—" her eyes cut briefly toward Koichi in clear warning "—is still at large, yes. But this new place is *way* more secure. There's an alarm system, and even security cameras. Plus there's that big old parking lot out front, and another one in back, both of them with lights on all night. And anyway, what kind of dumbass hits the same place twice?"

She had a point. Koichi drank from his water bottle while he considered.

He couldn't help noticing that Will watched his throat work as he swallowed, and turned his gaze away with a quick flash of mingled heat and guilt when Koichi lowered the bottle and licked his lips.

Interesting. And kind of sexy.

Will shifted from foot to foot. "What about the bog?"

Kimmy blinked at him. "What about it?"

"It's right there out back, you know?" Will scratched the side of his nose. "Anybody could hide in there. Right?"

"Not really." Koichi thought about it and amended himself. "Well. I suppose some people *could* hide in there, but not your average person. At least, not for long. It's a wilderness in the true sense of the word. Most people would get hopelessly lost in there the minute they got out of sight of the mall."

The worried crease stayed put between Will's eyes, but at least the corners of his mouth turned up. That little almost-smile made Koichi happy.

Kimmy rolled the chair backward, making the wheels squeak. "Bottom line: I don't think we're in any danger here. The thing that pisses me off is that Grammy's jewelry got stolen."

Will sucked on his bottom lip for a second before he spoke. It was so distracting Koichi completely missed what he said. "Sorry, what?"

Kimmy snickered like she knew all about Koichi's impure thoughts. Which she probably did.

Will, on the other hand, darted her a confused glance. God, he was clueless when it came to his own appeal. Was it wrong that Koichi found that so damn cute?

"I asked if that was the jewelry your grandparents found in your house when they first bought it." Will studied Koichi's face with curiosity shining in his eyes. "Because it sounds like those might've been some valuable pieces."

"I dunno. We never had them appraised, since we didn't want to sell." Koichi dug a thumb into the tense muscles at the back of his neck. "Anyway, yeah, it's pretty upsetting that some asshole stole them. It was bad enough when we thought they had been destroyed in the fire, but it's worse to think some thief took them."

"They took some of our stock too." Kimmy rose and stretched, both hands planted on the small of her back. "Nothing really valuable—"

"Because we don't *have* anything valuable," Koichi interrupted.

She shot him a cutting look. "Yeah, but it's still annoying."

"True." He let out a deep sigh. "I guess it could've been worse, though. We don't keep cash in the drawer, so at least they didn't get any money."

"Hmm." Will's lips pursed. His forehead scrunched. "Why you, though?"

Thinking about it only made Koichi angry. He laughed, sharp and bitter. "Who the fuck knows why people do what they do? They probably thought we'd be an easy target. And I guess they were right, in a way. They broke in without me even knowing it, even though I was right there in the back office." That fact bothered him. A lot.

Kimmy turned to gaze out the window overlooking the back parking lot. She didn't say anything, but Koichi got the distinct impression that she was thinking hard and didn't want to share what was going on in her head.

Which clearly made Will uncomfortable, judging by the way he shifted from foot to foot and hunched his shoulders. "Um. Anyhow, Koichi, I wanted to ask you about the test run into the bog. How do you feel about tomorrow night? The forecast is good, and we'll all be closed early since it's Sunday, so I figured it might be the perfect time. What d'you think? You still wanna go?"

Alone in the bog with Sexy Will tomorrow night? Yes, please, thank you, Jesus, said Koichi's libido. Since that wasn't socially acceptable to say with his words, he plastered on his most pleasant smile and nodded. "Sure, tomorrow's great. I'm in."

Will's grin lit up his face. "Fantastic. So, you want to just meet up here after work, or you want me to come get you at your house? 'Cause I can do that if you need some time to relax and get your stuff together before we head out."

"Naw, we can just leave from here. I'll bring my things to work with me."

"Cool." Will backed toward the door, still grinning. "Guess I'd better get back to the shop. See you later."

Koichi waved. "Later."

Kimmy murmured, "Bye," without turning around. She sounded uncharacteristically distracted.

Frowning, Koichi skirted the desk, walked up to his sister, and peered at her profile. She had the pinched, inward-focused expression that usually meant her brain was busy untangling a complicated problem.

He nudged her. "What're you working on in there, Nancy Drew?"

She didn't glare, or laugh, or react at all to the teasing nickname, meaning that whatever she had brewing in her head was Serious, with a capital *S*.

Serious Kimmy made him nervous. She tended to poke the proverbial bears, and Koichi had gotten clawed along with her too many times.

"I don't understand any of this." She turned to look at him, a deep furrow digging between her brows. "I mean, yeah, someone robbed us. People get robbed all the time. But why would they burn the place down? I don't get it."

He shrugged. "I don't know. Maybe they were mad that they couldn't find anything actually valuable to steal."

That got him a sour glance. "You're hilarious."

"Meaning I'm not, I guess."

She crossed her arms and stared at him. "Aren't you at all curious about it? You barely got out alive, after all."

That felt like a dig, though he didn't think she meant it that way. "Look, I know this won't make any sense to you. But that's one reason I *don't* want to think about it too hard. I have enough nightmares about the fire. I don't need any more."

Her expression softened a little. Her words didn't. "You're right. I don't understand."

He rummaged through his head, searching for a way to explain, and came up empty. Frustrated, he rubbed both hands over his face. "Okay, look. Maybe this guy's a pyro. Or maybe he knew I was there and wanted to cover up the robbery by making me think I'd started the fire by accident." Which had totally worked, whether it had been planned that way or not, but he wasn't unpacking *that* mental suitcase right now. "Hell, maybe he spilled his lighter fluid and started it by accident himself. I don't know. And I'm probably never *going* to know, because it's like Beauchamp told us at the station: the jewelry hasn't turned up, and there's practically zero evidence leading them to whatever sicko asshole did this."

Exhaustion rolled over him like a rogue wave. He perched on the edge of the desk and gazed out the window. "I get why you want to understand the why of it. But I'm tapped out when it comes to this thing. I just want to put it behind me and get on with my life." *Now that I know I didn't do it.*

For a few moments, nothing happened. He sat slump-shouldered on the desk, staring out the window while his sister studied him like a lab specimen.

Finally, Kimmy sat beside him, took his hand, and rested her head on his shoulder. "So. How about some of those chipotle chicken wraps from the coffee shop for lunch?"

One of these days, with any luck, he'd have a man to love. But nobody would ever know him like his sister did.

He couldn't decide if that was comforting, or just sad.

The first thing Will's research had taught him about Hunter's Bog was that getting to one of the few stretches of dry land large enough to set up a camp the size he wanted would mean boating in.

"No problem," Koichi said when Will broke the news Sunday morning. The two of them stood in the back parking lot ten minutes before opening, sipping coffee. "I mean, not for us, tonight. I have a boat we can use, and there's a public ramp not too far away."

That was a pleasant surprise. "Really?"

"Yeah. Lots of people go fishing out there. The waterways can handle boats easy enough, as long as you're not talking about anything too big." Koichi flashed a filthy grin. "Mine's just right. Slides in easy as pie."

Will blushed. Good Lord. He wasn't sure which was worse: Koichi's obvious double entendre, or his own thoroughly predictable reaction to it. "Well. That's . . . That's good, then."

The grin widened, Koichi's green eyes sparkling. "Of course, you might need a bigger one for what you want. Or maybe two. It might get tight in places, but—"

"For *fuck's* sake, T."

Will started and turned around. Kimmy stood in the doorway, hands on hips, scowling. He cranked his face into a smile and waved at her. "Morning, Kimmy."

"Hey, Will." Her sweet smile drained away, along with all her patience, when she turned to her brother. "We're opening in a few minutes, and there's still a shit-ton of stuff to do. Stop flirting and *get in here*." She spun on her heel and marched back inside.

Will and Koichi had both been raised in Southern homes. When a Southern woman aimed those three little words at you in that no-nonsense tone, you didn't argue. You got in there.

Will clapped Koichi on the back. "See you later."

"Yeah." Koichi trailed after his sister, walking backward. "Meet me here in the parking lot after work. You can follow me to my place, and we'll get my boat. We'll have to take your truck, though. I usually use Kimmy's. Or, well, she usually goes with me. My car doesn't have enough horsepower to pull a boat. Is that all right?"

"Of course. This is all for my business thing, after all. You're doing me a big enough favor letting me use your boat."

They exchanged a smile, and a feeling too big for words expanded in Will's chest. He floated into his shop convinced that he could do anything, be anything, endure anything, because Koichi was his friend.

Maybe more, whispered the part of him with clear sight and ambition beyond guilt.

He did his best to squash that voice, for a whole host of reasons. Not least of which was the part of him that had come here looking for Anthony.

But he left you. Didn't say a word, didn't tell you where he was going. Just left.

Will sighed. For months after that, he'd been frantic with worry, believing that Anthony was dead, or worse. Then he'd seen that picture—the single, random photo—that proved Anthony was alive and well, living in Baldwin County, Alabama. Or at least he'd been there at one point, which was a starting place if nothing else.

He doesn't love you anymore. If he ever did.

"He did. I know he did." Will rested his head on the wall of his office. Sweat rolled down his neck. Not from the heat. From nerves. From fear. He mopped it off and wiped his damp fingers on his jeans.

At this point, what they'd once had no longer mattered. He just wanted to *find* Anthony. To ask him what had happened. If he was all right. Why he'd left.

Especially the last question. Even if everything they'd once meant to each other was gone—even if it had never existed to anyone but Will—he needed to know why Anthony had abandoned him. Nothing else would ever make sense until he could answer that one question. What could Will's father have possibly threatened him with to make him take off without a word? Will needed an explanation.

Anthony was the only one left who could give Will the closure he needed.

He glanced at the clock. It was almost time to open. His angst would have to wait until later.

Squaring his shoulders, he shoved all his turmoil and uncertainty behind his smiling public mask and went to unlock the door.

Nine hours and fifteen minutes later, Will stood clutching the starboard rail of Koichi's boat while he navigated the twisting waterway deep into Hunter's Bog. Cypress trees overhung the narrow river, turning the water the color of strong black tea. The whole business made Will nervous as hell, though Koichi had assured him that the *Starbuck* only drew a little over a foot, even fully loaded.

And man, was it ever fully loaded now. The camp stove, tents, portable toilet, and food took up practically all the available storage space.

Will stifled a yelp when *Starbuck*'s bow missed another cypress knee by a hair. "Are you sure this boat'll make it to the campsite?"

Koichi sucked his cheeks in. Will could almost hear him counting to ten in his head. "For the dozenth time, *yes*. This model is made for shallow water. Kimmy and me take it out on the rivers around here all the time, and some of them are really shallow in spots." He cast Will a partly amused, mostly irritated look. "Will you relax? Go sit down. Have a beer or something."

It was tempting. And he needed to relax. But . . . "Do you know how to get there?"

"Oh my God. Yes, I know how to get there." This time, Koichi reached out and gave Will a playful shove. "As the captain of this vessel, I order you to go sit the fuck down already. You're getting on my nerves."

His smile said he was teasing, but Will knew he was also serious.

Will held up both hands in a gesture of surrender. "Okay. I'll get out of your hair."

"Thank you." Koichi jerked a thumb at the cooler wedged against the bench in the back. "Hand me a Dr. Pepper, would you?"

"Sure." Will opened the cooler, fished two drinks out of the ice, and handed one to Koichi. "Here."

"Thanks." Koichi popped his can open and drank several long swallows. "Mmm. Hits the spot."

Will settled onto the padded bench, opened his drink, and gulped a good quarter of it. The fizzy cold felt good in the still, sticky heat. He drew a deep breath. The air smelled like water and damp earth. Insects droned all around, creating a hypnotic white noise. Somewhere in the depths of the swamp, something hit the water with a *plop*. The westering sun created streaks of golden light and shadowy caverns beneath the trees. It lent the bog an aura of magic. As if Will and Koichi had wandered into a fairy tale.

"You can almost understand why people think this place is haunted." Koichi's voice was low and singsong, as if he'd forgotten Will was there and was talking to himself. "It has this kind of storybook feeling to it, sometimes." He cast a glance over his shoulder at Will. "You know what I mean?"

Since he thought it might freak Koichi out to know he'd practically read Will's mind, Will simply smiled and nodded. "I know exactly what you mean. Yes."

For a second, their gazes locked and held. Will's heart pounded so hard he was sure Koichi would hear it. Then Koichi blinked and faced forward again, and the moment broke.

While Koichi steered the *Starbuck* around yet another hairpin turn, Will sat there clutching his Dr. Pepper and trying to catch his breath. He hadn't felt as in sync with anyone since Anthony. The tangle of emotions that idea dragged up with it scared the crap out of him.

"Oh, hey. We're here."

Grateful to shake off the deep thoughts, Will rose and went to stand beside Koichi. Up ahead, the waterway widened and split, flinging two dark arms around a surprisingly large stretch of dry land. Cypress trees ran down to the water's edge on the left. To the right, a golden-brown beach cut a wide triangle through the grass and undergrowth toward the pines in the center of the island. The sun's leveling rays glittered on the little ripples washing against the sand.

Will grinned. "Wow. It's really pretty."

"Yeah, it is. Good thing, I guess, if you want to take paying customers out here." Koichi waited until they'd gotten within a few feet of the beach, then cut the motor. The boat's bow wedged into the sand. "C'mon. Let's get busy."

Will walked forward and hopped overboard. Koichi handed him the coolers of food and drink, their overnight bags, and the gear. Wrestling the camp stove off the boat and onto the beach took more doing, but they managed.

Working together, they rolled the stove up to a flat spot between the water and the woods, then started on the tents. Somewhat to Will's surprise, they got both tents set up and the tiki torches lit before darkness fell.

He walked around their small camp, searching for anything they'd missed, but saw nothing out of place. "All right. Everything looks good." He clapped Koichi on the back. "Nice job."

"Well, it's not exactly brain surgery." Koichi plopped into one of the sturdy canvas chairs, leaned over, and dug a bottle of hard cider out of the cooler. "What's for dinner? I'm hungry."

"Burgers, chips, and cookies for dessert."

"What?" Koichi groaned. "Man, I thought I was getting something awesome. You tricked me."

They hadn't known each other long, but Will had already learned to recognize when Koichi was teasing. He laughed. "Maybe you should've paid me."

"I'm paying in servitude. Apparently that doesn't count for much." Eyebrows arched, Koichi lifted his bottle to his lips and drank.

That shouldn't have been sexy, but it was. Damn it.

Will plastered on his best casual face while he lit the camp stove. "Your servitude is greatly appreciated. But you're still gonna have to make do with burgers tonight, since it's what I have. I couldn't get hold of the IPA I like for making your hush puppies. Sorry."

"No, you're not. Dirty liar." Shaking his head, Koichi pushed himself out of his chair and strolled over to Will's side. "All kidding aside, what can I do to help?"

"Nothing. Go sit back down and relax. I got it."

Koichi gave him a *yeah, right* look, unzipped the carrier, and started setting plates, napkins, and all the fixings on the portable table.

Watching him, a strange warmth dug into Will's chest, grew and expanded until he felt light-headed and breathless. He turned to the stove and concentrated on making his suddenly clumsy fingers lay the burger patties on the grill without dropping them.

He hoped like hell he could stop letting Koichi distract him like this. Otherwise, it was going to be a long night.

After dinner, they sat with their backs to the campfire and watched the fireflies glow in the darkness. Bugs, bullfrogs, and night birds kept up a constant, soothing music that drove all the lingering stress from Will's mind and made him feel more relaxed than he'd been in ages.

He linked his hands over his head and stretched. "This place is awesome. Let's stay here forever."

"I don't think so, Tarzan." Koichi slapped at his neck for about the dozenth time. "I mean, it's all nature-y and pretty and stuff, but at this rate the mosquitoes would drain me dry in a couple of days. I want to get back to civilization sooner rather than later." He smacked his knee, wiped his fingers on his shorts, reached over, and touched Will's wrist. "Not that I'm not enjoying myself, 'cause I am. It's a lot nicer out here than I thought it would be, and, well. You make everything more fun."

That tight feeling twisted in Will's chest again. Before he could think about what he was doing, he shifted, turned his arm, and clasped Koichi's hand in his.

Time stopped. They sat there, palm pressed to palm, staring into each other's eyes. Will's heartbeat hammered in his ears. He wondered if he wore the same stunned, can-this-really-be-happening expression as Koichi. Even more, he wondered if Koichi felt the same spark as he did.

Koichi's grip tightened. He leaned in, lips parting, and Will's heart turned over.

A bright light shone through the trees deeper in the swamp, accompanied by the growl of a motor. Startled, Will let go of Koichi's hand. They both stood at the same time, backing away from the fire as if to hide in the shadows.

Koichi drew close to Will, and they stood stock-still, listening as what was clearly a motorboat of some sort puttered along a waterway somewhere farther in the interior of the bog. The boat's big spotlight turned this way and that, as if looking for something. Will heard the faint sound of voices buried in the rumble of the motor, but couldn't make out what they were saying.

Gradually, the light became fainter and farther away, and the noises faded. Will didn't dare to move until the spotlight blended in with the fireflies and he could no longer hear the boat's motor. He drew a deep breath and blew it out along with most of the tension in his shoulders. "What. The hell."

"No idea." Koichi rubbed his neck, his face thoughtful. "Probably hunters, I guess."

"Hunters? What're they hunting at night?"

"Alligators, most likely."

Will frowned. "Is that legal?"

"You're asking me?" Koichi lifted both arms in a universal *who knows* gesture. "I have no fucking clue. But I know people like to hunt gators, and I know they do it at night. Alligator tail's damn good meat."

It sounded like a great dish to serve on a glamping expedition. Will opened his mouth to ask where he could get some, how best to cook it, and how to keep the gators away from the camp. He hadn't even thought of that before. Then something rustled in the undergrowth on the other side of the camp fire. He looked, and his words died on his tongue.

A face peered back at him from the gloom, wan and ghostly in the outer reaches of the light. A face he thought he knew, though he hadn't seen it in two years.

Anthony.

CHAPTER 6

Will's universe shrank down to an Anthony-shaped singularity. For the first time, he realized he'd never truly expected to find the man he'd lost. Seeing him here, in a trackless swamp in Southern Alabama, was a shock to the system.

He took a step forward. Anthony vanished.

No. God, no.

"No." Will skirted the fire, striding toward the trees. "No! Come back!"

"Will? What're you doing?"

Koichi. Shit.

Will ducked into his tent and grabbed his flashlight. "Stay here."

"What? Where're you going?"

Will hated to ignore him, but there wasn't time for questions and answers. He plunged into the forest. "Anthony! It's me, Will. Please, don't run away."

For a second, Koichi's following footsteps halted. Will could almost feel his surprise, and his uncertainty. Then the crackle of shoes on pine straw resumed, and Will knew Koichi was still with him.

It was comforting, though he knew he shouldn't drag Koichi out into the wilderness.

He can go or not. His choice.

All of which flitted through Will's mind between one footstep and the next without slowing him down. He kept going, clambering over fallen trees, muscling his way through thick patches of undergrowth, splashing across trickling creeks. "Anthony?" He swung his flashlight side to side, looking for any trace of the man he knew was here somewhere. "Where are you?"

Out of sight ahead, something went *snap*. Will heard something heavy moving through close-packed brush in the dark. Heart in his throat, he shone his light toward the noise. He caught a swift movement and saw a flash of white. A deer. Frustrated, he jogged onward.

Behind him, Koichi cursed. "Will, c'mon, stop."

"Go back if you want. I have to find him." Will slowed down enough to half turn and hold the flashlight out to Koichi. "You can take the light."

Koichi glared at him. "I'm not going back without you, idiot. We should *both* go back." He turned in a circle, frowning. "If we still can."

"What're you talking about? We haven't come *that* far." Will stumbled directly from a tangle of thorny vines into another stream. This one was deeper than the others, wetting his legs halfway to the knee. The water tugged at him with a current stronger than he'd expected, forcing him to slow down so he wouldn't lose his balance. "Fuck. Anthony! Wait!"

Koichi's sigh was loud and ripe with aggravation. "Christ almighty." He sloshed into the water behind Will. "Hey. Hey!"

His shout cut through the thick, humid air, scaring the bugs and frogs into silence and stopping Will in his tracks a couple of feet short of the other side of the stream. He turned the flashlight beam on Koichi. "Are you all right?"

"All right? Are you fucking *kidding* me?" Koichi flung his arms wide. "Look around, genius. We're standing in a fucking *creek* in the middle of a fucking *swamp*, and in case you didn't notice, we are *fucking lost*. Because you had to go chasing after someone who *wasn't. Fucking. There.*" He laughed. It was the aural equivalent of stepping on a glass sliver in a rug—shocking, cutting, painful. "No, Will. I'm not fucking all right. And neither are you, even if you don't realize it yet."

Will forced himself to stand still for a moment, to watch and listen. The bog was quiet, except for the normal sounds of a summer night which were beginning to return all around them. He couldn't see anything moving in the dark, or feel the prickling sense of a hidden presence nearby.

He's gone. I lost him.

All his energy drained away. He dragged himself out of the water, sat down in the weeds on the other side, and put his head in his hands. He let the flashlight fall to the ground. Eventually, he'd have to get up and let Koichi take him back to the camp. But he couldn't face it right now.

Koichi sighed again. Will heard him wade through the water and onto the shore, felt the warmth of his slight body when he sat next to Will with their arms pressed together.

"I'm sorry I yelled at you," Koichi said after a few tense seconds. "I know you only moved here to find him. So, of course if you thought you saw him, you'd want to follow." He hesitated the space of a breath. "I guess I'd've done the same thing, if it was me."

Will smiled, in spite of the dread coiling in his gut. He was grateful that Koichi wanted to make him feel better, when he had every reason to keep reading him the riot act.

He tilted his head sideways and down, touching his forehead to Koichi's sweat-damp hair because he couldn't help it. "I'm sorry I ran off like that. I just . . ." He searched for a good reason for his behavior, and came up short. "I don't know. I swear to God I saw his face, Koichi. I did." Didn't he? That face had been so pale. Thinner than he remembered. And the way it had just vanished . . . But he'd been so sure. "But it couldn't have been real, could it?"

Koichi was quiet for a moment. He half turned his face toward Will's. Laid a palm on Will's cheek, making his heart beat faster. "Honestly? I don't know. But I don't see how. I saw you stare at something, and I looked, but I didn't see anything at all. I didn't hear anything." He tilted his head until his warm breath touched Will's lips. "I'm really sorry. I know how bad you want to find Anthony."

The sound of that name in Koichi's voice started a riot of confused emotions inside Will. He'd loved Anthony with his whole being. But Anthony had left him. And Koichi was here, warm and smart and funny and cute and bluntly truthful, and God, Will wanted him. But how could he when Koichi himself was sitting there in the dark with mud on his face, reminding him that he'd come here to find Anthony?

Conflicted, he turned away, breaking the uncomfortably intimate contact. "Are we really lost?"

Silence. Koichi breathed hard and fast beneath the drone of the crickets. Will wondered if he'd screwed up permanently.

When Koichi finally answered, it was a huge relief. "I hate to say so, but I think we are." He leaned across Will, snatched up the flashlight, and switched it off. "Look around. Can you see the campfire?"

At first, Will thought he couldn't only because his eyes weren't yet adjusted to the darkness. But after a couple of minutes had passed, when the half-moon filtered through the canopy to illuminate the running water and the gently swaying Spanish moss hanging from the cypress limbs, he had to admit he couldn't see a damn thing that looked like firelight. Not even the tiniest flicker.

He groaned. "Oh shit, Koichi. *Shit*. We're *lost*."

"Yeah." Koichi patted his arm. "It's okay, big guy. We've got our phones. We'll just . . . you know. GPS it. Or call somebody. It'll be fine."

"Right. Okay." Will's rising hope deflated when he patted his pockets and realized he'd left his phone back at camp. Fuck, fuck, fuck, fuck. "Um. I don't have my phone." He studied Koichi's face in the moonlight, thinking it was a good idea to not use the flashlight for now. Save the batteries. "Do you have yours?"

"Yep. Hang on." Koichi shifted onto one hip, leaning his weight against Will's side to fish his phone out of his shorts pocket. He thumbed it on. The screen bathed his features in cold white light. He stabbed at it for a few seconds, then scowled. "I'm not getting any signal out here. Or any GPS."

Guilt and fear pulled at Will's body like a physical force. He wrapped his arms around himself, doing his best to stifle the panic rising inside him. He'd screwed up before, but this time took the proverbial cake. If they survived this, Koichi would probably never speak to him again.

"Hey. Will." Koichi laid a hand on Will's shoulder and leaned over to peer into his face. His head was nothing but a silhouette in the darkness. "Look, let's not dwell on how we got here, okay? Let's just concentrate on getting out. That's what's important."

He had a point. Will shut his eyes and visualized shoving his fear behind a locked door. *If you panic, you die. Calm down and use your brain.*

He opened his eyes. "You're right. Give me a few minutes to figure out the lay of the land, and maybe I can work out how to get us back to the camp."

Koichi drew away. The moonlight glimmered on his smile. "My hero."

Will was grateful for the darkness hiding his blush. He pushed to his feet, brushed the grass and sand from his shorts, and scooped up his flashlight. "Come on. I'm afraid the first thing we have to do is go back across this creek."

"Yeah. I figured." Koichi rose and shoved his phone in his pocket. "Lead on, Ranger Rick."

Shaking his head, Will switched on the light and aimed the beam at the water. He had some skill in wilderness survival, but he'd never been in this sort of environment before moving to Alabama. He hoped like hell he could get them both out of this mess.

Koichi lost track of how long they spent fighting their way through underbrush and slogging across shallow, muddy creeks. It was slow going. Will moved with cautious, deliberate steps, stopping every few seconds to peer at the ground, or turn off the light and stare at the sky. Koichi didn't ask what he was doing. Looking for moss on the north sides of rocks and checking the position of the stars, probably. It wasn't like Koichi knew anything about finding his way in the wild.

Of course, he hadn't realized Will knew anything about it either. He found this whole rugged-tracker thing uncomfortably sexy.

Ahead of him, Will stopped, planted both hands on his lower back and stretched. "Damn. Stupid bog."

Koichi resisted the urge to hug him. "You having trouble?"

"Yeah. I've found my way through the desert or the woods more than once, but a swamp's a whole different thing." Will turned, guilt stamped all over his face. "I'm really sorry, Koichi. If I hadn't gone haring off like that, we wouldn't be lost. I wish I could take it back."

Technically, he was right. But who could stay mad at him when he stood there looking so damn pitiful? Not Koichi.

Calling himself a sucker the whole time, he closed the distance between them, took Will's free hand and squeezed. "Yeah, you acted like an idiot. But so what? We're all allowed our idiot moments." He grinned. "For whatever it's worth, I forgive you."

The relief that washed over Will's features made Koichi feel bad for ever having been angry in the first place, even though he knew he'd had valid reasons to be mad.

Will clasped Koichi's hand hard. "It's worth a lot, believe me. Thank you."

For a second, Koichi's head swam. He'd never wanted to kiss anyone more in his life. But it wasn't the time or place. He knew for a solid fact that he wouldn't be able to stop at a kiss. Not as long as Will was into it. And unless he'd read the signals totally wrong, he figured Will would be *way* into it.

Since neither of them could afford for Will to get distracted right now, Koichi forced himself to drop Will's hand and step back. He was standing there fumbling for something to say when a metallic glint caught the tail of his eye.

He picked his way forward through a tangle of vines and fallen branches, trying to keep sight of whatever it was he'd spotted. It flashed through the trees like a quarter hanging from a string. "Will? Do you see that?"

The bracken rustled as Will stepped up beside him. "See what?"

"That." The thing gleamed again, and Koichi pointed. "Right there. Like something metal. See?"

"Oh. Yeah." Will leaned his head next to Koichi's. "Whatever it is, it has to be manmade."

"Meaning it might be useful?"

"Exactly." Will grinned at him. "Come on."

They pushed through the bushes and weeds together. Will's flashlight kept them out of the worst of the thorns and puddles, and held them to their path by shining on the bit of mysterious metal.

After a few minutes, Koichi could see its shape—long and thin, obviously a railing. His pulse pounded hard. "It's a boat, Will. Oh my God." He started running, kicking up a sandy soil now that the undergrowth had thinned.

Will was right behind him. When the flashlight's beam picked out *Starbuck* painted in royal blue on the side of the boat, they both whooped. Koichi turned and flung himself into Will's arms. Will dropped the flashlight and spun him around, laughing. "We did it, T, we fucking did it!"

"Hell yeah, we did." Koichi looked into Will's smiling face, his shining brown eyes, and damn it, he simply could not resist. Planting both hands on Will's cheeks, he tilted his head and kissed him.

Will made a tiny, helpless sound. His lips parted, softly, gently. Then his tongue slid against Koichi's, and everything soft and gentle burned away in a firestorm of need.

How they got to Will's tent, Koichi never could exactly remember. But they ended up there, snatching rough kisses in between the frantic removal of soggy shoes, muddy shorts, and filthy T-shirts.

They didn't make it all the way to the cot. Will took them to the canvas floor, kicking off his shorts and underwear while Koichi straddled his hips. He gripped Koichi's hair in one fist and his right ass cheek in the other, eating at his mouth like a starving dog.

Koichi shifted enough to worm a hand between their bodies and wrap his fingers around Will's rigid cock. God almighty, he felt good—big, hard, hot, and alive in Koichi's palm. He tightened his grip, and bit his lip when Will groaned.

"Oh fuck." Will moaned and squirmed between Koichi's thighs. "Jesus God, I . . . I'm . . . Ohhh my God."

Oh yeah. That's the stuff. Koichi swooped in and bit Will's neck, relishing his own power. He pulled his hand out of the way and rocked his hips, a slow and deliberate movement, rubbing his prick against Will's. The heat and hardness shot electricity along his skin. *Nownownow!* hollered his primitive brain. *Come now, nownownow!* Gritting his teeth, he mentally counted the shop's stock of laundry soap until the part of him that was good at sex could gain control of the part that just wanted to rut like a rabbit.

Still seesawing his hips, he leaned down to put his lips to Will's ear. "Goddamn, you're hot. I wanna fuck you."

A tremor shook Will's body. "Oh Jesus."

That sounded like a *Jesus, yes*, not a *Jesus, no*. But something nagged at the back of Koichi's mind. Something they were missing.

Something being driven away by the friction and the man-smell and the *Comecomecome* screaming in his lizard-brain.

"Rubbers," Will gasped. "Don't have any."

That was it. No condoms. Or lube, for that matter.

Koichi laid his sweaty face in the curve of Will's neck. "Fuck a *fucking* duck."

Will laughed, hoarse and breathless. "Probably got that option. There's a few out there."

Snickering, Koichi smacked his hip. "Shut up. Pervert."

"You brought it up." Will tugged Koichi's hair, lifting his head. Grinning, he used the hand still planted on Koichi's ass to shove their groins together so hard Koichi's eyes crossed. "This works for me."

In his head, Koichi agreed. Since his words had decided to stop coming out his mouth, he indicated his enthusiasm for that plan by thrusting his prick into Will's. Then again, and again. Will's grin dissolved, leaving his expression soft, open, and vulnerable.

Watching him like this was too much. Too intense. So Koichi bent and kissed him, deep and rough and urgent, until Will was arching under him, holding his butt in an iron grip to keep the pressure on. And that was intense too, so much that his skin felt too small to contain it, but at least he was spared the intimacy of meeting Will's unfiltered gaze. He didn't think he could handle that. It would burn him alive.

Will's breath stuttered. "Oh, oh fu . . ." His voice dissolved into wordless keening, his fingers tightened to the point of pain on Koichi's rear and in his hair, and slick warmth spread between their bodies.

Jolted by the sudden heat of Will's release, orgasm surprise-attacked Koichi like a raptor. He came with a full-body shudder, his mouth slack and panting against Will's, his cock still pressed to Will's, both of them wet and sticky and spent.

He collapsed onto Will's damp chest. "Wow. Holy fuck."

"Yeah. I needed that." Will let out an honest-to-God giggle. He sounded loopy and sex-drunk and adorable, and Koichi's insides went gooey.

Because he still couldn't face the thought of looking into Will's eyes, he cuddled closer, rubbing his cheek on Will's chest hair. Now that he was coming down off the O-high, he started to notice what rough shape he was in. Sweat, dirt, and swamp water coated him head to foot, and he'd managed to gather quite a collection of scratches on his arms and legs. Also, he was pretty sure a mosquito had just bitten him on the ass.

He mustered enough energy to reach back and scratch the itchy spot. "Bugs're eating me, Will."

"Mmm. I don't blame 'em." He gave Koichi's butt a lazy squeeze. "I'd like to eat you too."

Smiling, Koichi planted a kiss on Will's collarbone. "Sweet talker."

"I try." More butt-kneading. Will seemed to have a thing for that. "We ought to get cleaned up. Don't know about you, but I was already a mess. Now I'm a *sticky* mess."

"Me too. But I don't wanna get up. It's comfy here."

"Except for the mud. And the sweat. And the love juice."

Koichi laughed. "Oh my God, you did *not* just say that."

"Love. Juice." Will punctuated each word with a sharp smack to Koichi's ass. "Get used to it, 'cause I do believe you're gonna be getting my love juice on a regular basis from now on."

Something caught hard at Koichi's heart. With time and banter protecting him now, he felt safe lifting his head and peering into Will's flushed, dirty, smiling face. "I like that plan."

"So do I." Will's grin widened. Without warning, he grasped Koichi under the armpits and lifted him into the air.

Koichi managed not to squeal in surprise, but it was a near thing. "What the hell are you doing?"

"Helping you up." Still holding Koichi like some kind of giant rag doll, Will ratcheted himself into a sitting position, folded his legs, and struggled to his feet with a complete lack of grace. He set Koichi down, finally, and mopped a new crop of sweat drops from his forehead. "Shit. That looked a lot more badass in my head."

The lightness in Koichi's chest grew and expanded until his heart labored and he could barely breathe. Robbed of words, he wound his arms around Will's waist and pressed close. Will laid a hand on his cheek, tilted his head, and kissed him, a slow, lazy kiss that sent tendrils of sweet heat through Koichi's body.

Good grief, he was in so much trouble.

Unsurprisingly, neither of them thought to set an alarm, meaning they slept *way* later than they'd intended to and didn't leave their campsite until almost nine. Koichi figured it would've been even later if Will wasn't a born early bird.

The journey back to the public boat landing was quiet and tense. Koichi was pushing *Starbuck* as fast as he dared, and all his attention was focused on guiding her safely through the shallow, treacherous water. Will perched on the seat beside him, tapping one heel on the floor and gnawing his lower lip. Nervous as all get out, obviously.

Not that Koichi blamed him. Kimmy was going to give them both hell for being late. Him especially, since he'd left her to open up alone without warning, and made her worry. He wondered how many times she'd tried to call him already.

Sure enough, as soon as *Starbuck* got in cell-tower range, his phone started beeping at him. He sighed. "Shit."

Will shot him a wry smile. "Might as well call her now and let her yell at us. She's got the right."

"What do you mean, 'us'?"

"Koichi."

"I know, I know." Steeling himself, he pulled his phone from his shorts pocket, swiped it on, and brought up the messages. "Jesus, she's called me fourteen times in the last three hours."

Will's eyebrows drew together. "Something's wrong."

"Yeah." Worried now, Koichi throttled down and called her.

Kimmy picked up after the first ring. "Fuck, Koichi, where've you *been*?"

Now didn't seem like the time to get into the whole getting lost in the swamp business. "We overslept. There's no cell reception out there. What—"

"Where are you now? Are you almost back?"

"We're a few minutes out from Lain Park." He steered around a wide bend. Two women fishing from a flatboat ahead scowled at him. He throttled down again. "Kimmy, what happened? Are you okay?" A terrible thought struck him. "Oh no, did something happen to Grammy?"

"No, everyone's fine." She breathed into the phone for a second, loud and shaky. "There was another break-in."

Shit. "The shop?"

"No. Your house."

CHAPTER 7

A wave of cold washed down Koichi's spine. "My house?"
Will laid a hand on his knee. *What?* he mouthed.

Koichi shook his head and whispered, "Wait."

"Mrs. Dooley saw two people running out your back door around four this morning," Kimmy said. "So she called the police. The officers who showed up said the lock was broken and the whole place was ransacked."

"Oh my God." Bile rose in Koichi's throat. He swallowed hard. "Did they take anything? Do you know?"

"Yeah, I've already been over there and gave it a quick look. They took the TV, your laptop, and your PlayStation. I don't know about anything else. The place is a wreck."

Ouch. "Goddamn it."

"I know. I'm sorry, hon. Hang on." She said something Koichi couldn't make out to someone on the other end. Probably a customer. "I need to go. There's a lot of customers here this morning. You need to head straight to your place. Detective Beauchamp ought to still be there. He'll want to talk to you."

"Okay. Thanks, sis. Love you."

"Love you too, T." She hesitated a moment. "I'm glad y'all are okay. I was worried."

She cut the connection before he could say *I know.*

Will slid to the edge of his seat. "Koichi, what happened?"

"Someone broke into my house. My neighbor saw them leaving and called the cops." Good thing Mrs. Dooley had to get up insanely early for her job, or Koichi would've walked unprepared right into the middle of it. The thought creeped him out. "I have to go straight home to talk to the detective. I'm sorry, Will. I know that's gonna mean you have to open even later today."

Will brushed that off with a wave of his hand. "Don't worry about it. I'll take you home, and I'll stay with you."

Okay, that was a surprise. "You don't need to do that."

"I know. I *want* to." Will squeezed Koichi's thigh, where his hand still rested. "It's not a problem for me. Let me help."

How could he say no? Smiling, he clasped Will's hand in his. "Okay. Thanks."

Will flashed a grin, leaned over, and planted a swift kiss on his lips. The touch was new enough to thrill, yet already familiar enough to comfort. Koichi couldn't quite decide how to feel about that.

Getting back to the park and hauling the boat out felt like it took forever. The drive to his place was a whole new forever. By the time they pulled up in front of his house, he was jumpy as a mouse in an aerie.

Yellow crime-scene tape blocked the front door, and a uniformed officer stood on the front porch looking stern. Koichi's stomach rolled. He opened the door and hopped down from the cab of Will's truck.

Will put a soothing hand on his shoulder as they crunched up the gravel walkway together. He didn't say anything, but his presence calmed Koichi's nerves. He cut Will a grateful sidelong smile.

The cop guarding the door came forward to block their way up the porch steps. "I'm sorry, but no one can come in right now. This is a crime scene."

He's just doing his job. No yelling. "I'm Koichi McNab. This is my house. Is Detective Beauchamp here?"

The officer's mouth formed an *Oh*. "Yeah, he's inside. Hang on, I'll get him." The man turned, trotted back to the door, opened it, and leaned inside. "Hal! The owner's here."

A few seconds later, Beauchamp stepped onto the porch. He strode forward, his hand out. "Mr. McNab. I'm really sorry to have to see you again under these circumstances."

"Me too." Koichi shook the detective's hand. "Do you have any idea who might've done this?"

Beauchamp shook his head. "I was going to ask *you* that. Your neighbor's pretty sure it was two men, but other than that she wasn't able to make out details."

"Oh." Koichi rubbed his chin. "Why wouldn't it be just random thieves?"

"It could be, of course." The detective mopped sweat from his brow. "But random thieves don't generally take the time to ransack the place they hit. They're in and out as quickly as possible. This feels more like someone looking for something they have reason to believe they might find here."

Koichi found that idea exceedingly uncomfortable. He rubbed his arms, trying to rid himself of the sudden case of goose bumps. "I can't think of anybody who would do that."

"Except maybe whoever hit your shop," Will said.

Good grief. That made Koichi feel positively hunted. He resisted the urge to turn around and look behind him.

Beauchamp narrowed his eyes. "What makes you say so, Mister . . . Hood, right?"

Koichi bit the insides of his cheeks so his big mouth wouldn't get him in trouble. Leave it to the law to make it sound like Will had said something suspicious rather than sensible.

Will's cheeks flushed, but he stayed calm. "Will Hood, that's right. And it only seems logical, doesn't it? I mean, whoever robbed the shop might've thought they'd find something valuable here at the house. It just stands to reason, I think."

Beauchamp turned his blank cop-face to Koichi. "Do you have any valuables they might've been after? Anything you might've had hidden? Something they might have had reason to know about, or have heard about somehow?"

"Umm . . ." Koichi mentally sorted through all the various junk he'd collected over the years, and all the other stuff left behind after Grampa died and Grammy moved in with his parents. He had lots of things that were precious to him and to his family, but very little of any objective value, and nothing that anyone else would know about. "I can't think of anything." A distinctly uncomfortable idea hit him, and he moved closer to Will because it felt safer there. "Maybe they thought I had more of Grammy's old jewelry."

Will slipped his arm around Koichi's waist. "Yeah. I mean, whoever robbed the shop burned it down to cover up that theft."

"Maybe," Beauchamp pointed out. "We don't know the motive for sure."

Technically, he was right. But privately, Koichi thought Will had nailed it. "Whatever their motive was for burning down our shop, they definitely took that jewelry. So I guess it's possible they were looking for more." He mulled it over. "And that probably points to someone local, I think, because everyone around here knows this was Grammy's house, and a lot of her old stuff is still here." That didn't sit well with him at all. He knew almost everyone in Duchene. If someone he'd exchanged small talk with in town every day had done this to him . . .

Will rubbed a hand up and down his back. "It wouldn't have had to be anyone you know personally. They could've just talked to the locals and found out what they wanted to know."

"I guess." Koichi glanced at him. "Thanks for trying to make me feel better, in any case."

Beauchamp pursed his lips. Disapproval peeked through the cracks of his professional mask, but whatever his thoughts about Koichi and Will's relationship, he kept them to himself. "How long have you been in town, Mr. Hood?"

"A few weeks. I moved here from Houston." Will blinked, surprise flowing over his features. "Wait, you don't think I had anything to do with this, do you?"

"Will was camping with me last night," Koichi said before Beauchamp could answer. "I'll personally vouch for him. He was still in Houston when our old shop burned down. There's absolutely no way he was involved in *any* of this."

The detective held up both hands. "Slow down, son, I never said he was. It's my job to cover all the bases. In any case, so far we don't have any evidence linking the two robberies. So you'll have to understand if I want to question the guy who seems to think they're related."

It made sense, from the detective's point of view. But Koichi couldn't believe Will was involved. He crossed his arms. "I thought he had a good point. Just 'cause there's no evidence yet doesn't mean he's wrong, you know."

Beauchamp sighed the sigh of the deeply put out. "We should be finished here soon. You can wait if you like, or go do something else and I'll call you when you're allowed in. I'll warn you: it's a mess in there. If you need help with the cleanup, I know of a service that's really good. I can give you their number."

Koichi's heart sank. "No, that's okay. I'd rather do it myself."

"I'll help," Will offered. "No need to tackle it all alone."

Koichi smiled. "Thank you. I appreciate that."

Nobody's eyes ought to shine like that at the prospect of cleaning somebody else's wrecked house, but Will's sure did. Koichi didn't understand it, but he liked it.

Will dropped his arm from around Koichi's waist. "Why don't we unhitch the boat, then go get some breakfast? I don't know about you, but I'm starved."

At the mention of food, Koichi's stomach gurgled. They hadn't eaten yet, what with the scramble to break camp that morning and get back. "Good idea. Detective, you have my cell number, right?"

He nodded. "Y'all go on. I'll call you when we're done."

"Okay. Thanks."

Koichi turned and followed Will down the steps. As they walked toward the truck, Will held his hand palm down toward Koichi, the gesture subtle but unmistakable. Koichi hesitated for a second, then grinned and took Will's hand.

Behind them, the cop at the door mumbled something that sounded like "fuckin' fags." Beauchamp shushed him. Will rolled his eyes, and Koichi stifled a laugh.

He'd walked around town with other men before. He'd dated plenty. It wasn't like his sexuality was a secret. But for some reason, with Will he felt free.

He could get used to that.

The second Will walked through Koichi's front door later that morning, he made up his mind to move in with him. Not because it was a fabulous place—though he could see it was normally very nice, when it wasn't trashed—but because whoever had ransacked it was clearly dangerous. No way was he leaving Koichi alone if there was any chance that these people might come back.

"Oh my God, Will." Koichi stepped over a coffee table lying on its side and plucked a curved piece of thick blue glass from the floor in front of the fireplace. "They broke Grammy's vase. It belonged to her mother." He peered at Will with anguish stamped all over his face. "How am I gonna tell her this? She's going to be so upset."

"I think she'll mostly be relieved that you weren't home, since I'm sure you're more important to her than a vase."

"Yeah. Still." Koichi picked up the pieces of the vase and set them on the mantel, then plopped onto the sofa, shoulders slumped. "Look at this place. I don't even know where to start."

Will's heart ached. He wove his way through the photos, overturned furniture, and miscellaneous bits of Koichi's life strewn across the hardwood floor and went to sit beside him. "We could start in here. Or we could start in your bedroom, if you'd rather."

Koichi arched an eyebrow at him. "Are you propositioning me?"

He hadn't been, at least not on purpose, but . . . "Do you want to be propositioned?" He grinned.

A filthy smile spread over Koichi's face. "Maybe it's weird right now, but yeah. I do."

Heart galloping, Will leaned in and pressed a soft, slow kiss to Koichi's mouth. Then another, and another. God, he loved kissing this man. He could spend long hours doing nothing else. Koichi buried both hands in Will's hair, and Will moaned.

"We really shouldn't." Koichi nipped Will's lower lip, a light, quick pain. "We ought to get started on this mess."

"Probably." Will slid a hand up the inside of Koichi's thigh, underneath his baggy shorts. "Lie down."

Koichi laughed, low and breathless. "Bossy." He claimed a hard kiss, then stretched out on his back on the sofa, both arms above his head, green eyes hooded and glittering. His half smile said, *What now, big talker?*

Will met the implied challenge by yanking off Koichi's still-damp hiking shoes and tossing them on the floor, then flipping open the button on his shorts. He pulled down the zipper and stopped, grasping the waistband, watching Koichi's flushed face. Last night had been rushed. Frantic. Now? He wanted to take his time. To look his fill, in the full light of day.

Koichi wriggled his hips. "Sometime today, maybe?"

Warmth flooded Will's insides. He couldn't remember the last time he'd had so much *fun* with sex. Grinning, he eased the shorts and underwear over Koichi's butt, down his legs, and off. He let them drop to the floor and drank in the sight of Koichi's flat belly, his lean legs, his uncut cock and tightly drawn balls.

"God, you're gorgeous." Will leaned down, buried his nose in Koichi's groin, and breathed deep. "I love how you smell." He got his mouth around Koichi's left testicle, turning whatever smart-mouth thing he'd been about to say into a gasp-and-groan combo that went straight to Will's prick. Feeling smug, he sucked gently for a moment before letting go. "I love how you taste."

"Christ almighty." Koichi tugged on Will's hair. "Quit it. You're gonna set me off before you even get naked."

The mental picture intrigued Will more than it probably should have. "I don't know. I kind of like that idea."

The shiver that ran through Koichi's thighs spoke volumes. "Later. Right now I want you to take off your fucking clothes, you evil, evil person."

"Okay. If you insist." Will took the time to rub his stubbly chin on the bend where Koichi's leg met his groin, resulting in a squeal and a painful yank on his hair.

Worth it, he thought, rising to his knees and peering at Koichi's glazed eyes and flaming cheeks.

He held Koichi's gaze as he pulled his shirt over his head and threw it aside. He tried to do the same while he undid his shorts and shoved them down to his knees, but Koichi seemed more interested in staring at his cock instead.

Not that Will could talk. He liked to stare at Koichi's junk too.

He tried to think of a sexy way to get his shorts and shoes all the way off, but nothing came to mind, so he plunked down on his ass and wrestled the whole business over his feet in a giant tangle. It joined the growing pile on the floor. That done, he leaned over and hauled Koichi up by his T-shirt. "Off."

Laughing, Koichi helped Will get the shirt over his head and toss it away. "There. Happy?"

"Yes." Will ran both hands down Koichi's smooth chest, letting his thumbs catch on the little pink nipples. "Oh, yes. Very happy."

"Me too." Koichi traced light, feathery touches across Will's bare sides, over his abs, down to his groin. Ran his fingertips up Will's cock and over the leaking slit, sending shockwaves through his blood. "You know what I want?"

Will opened his mouth to speak. Koichi cupped his balls in one hand and grasped his prick in the other, and Will's brain decided speech wasn't happening right now. He shook his head.

Koichi kissed Will's lips, light and quick. "I want you to suck my cock. I've dreamed about it." He kissed him again, tongue flicking out to taste the corner of Will's mouth. "Please?"

The thought made Will's mouth water. He tried to answer with words and couldn't, so he pried Koichi's fingers off his balls and pushed him down onto the sofa cushions.

Koichi lay back and spread his legs, watching Will with slitted, glittering eyes. He didn't say anything, but his flushed skin and quick, shallow breaths told Will he wasn't the only one on the edge.

Will smoothed his palms down the insides of Koichi's slender thighs. His skin was warm, soft, and firm, unblemished except for a crescent-shaped scar a few inches below his left hip. Will brushed his thumb over the shiny, raised spot. "Where'd this come from?"

"Shrapnel. Kimmy, our friend Lester, and me had a fireworks accident when we were twelve." Koichi reached out and touched Will's fingers with his. "Will, c'mon. I'm getting blue balls here."

Chuckling, Will bent and pressed a tender kiss to Koichi's scar. Koichi's thigh trembled. Encouraged, Will trailed kisses along the taut tendon to Koichi's pubic hair. God, he smelled good, ripe with sweat and arousal. Will swiped his tongue over Koichi's balls, gathering the dense, salty flavor. In return, he got a low, throaty moan that sparked along his nerve endings like lightning.

Will had no particular attachment to sucking cock. He liked it all right, had never had a problem performing the act, but it didn't feel like a loss if he missed a chance. Which made his eagerness to get Koichi's prick in his mouth sort of puzzling. But there was no mistaking how he felt right now. He was, as the saying went, gagging for it.

Been a loooong time, you know.

He silently told his inner monologue to shut the fuck up, then opened wide and swallowed Koichi's cock.

"Oh God." Koichi tangled his fingers in Will's hair. His hips lifted a little, then fell back, shaking, and Will knew he was making a mighty effort not to thrust. "God, that's good. Shit."

Mmm. That breathless voice was nice. But Will was going for nonverbal. He relaxed his throat and took Koichi deep. Deeper. Held for a moment. Pulled off slowly, sucking hard, teasing the slit with his tongue before doing it all again.

This time, there were no words, but the noise Koichi made clearly said, *You are a master of fellatio, and I am your helpless victim.*

Hell, yes.

Since Koichi seemed into it, Will kept up the rhythm he'd started. Down, hold, up, gently rolling Koichi's balls in one hand. When Koichi's pleasure sounds went from languid to frantic and his legs started to tremble, Will got his hand into it, stroking him hard, until Koichi cried out and came in Will's mouth.

Oh, Jesus. Will shut his eyes, breathed and swallowed, and did his best to hang on to the ragged ends of his control. He didn't want to come like this—on the sofa cushions, untouched, like a fucking teenager getting his cherry popped.

He knelt there sucking at Koichi's softening prick until Koichi squirmed and shoved him away. "Too much."

He grinned. He was always super sensitive after orgasm too. Rising onto his knees, he took his still-hard cock in one hand. "What about this?"

Koichi's eyes gleamed with wicked intent. "Oh, I know what to do with *that*, all right." He rose and claimed a swift kiss. "Stay right there."

Will watched, spellbound, as Koichi bent and wrapped those beautiful lips around his cock. Koichi slid down, then down some more, until he'd taken Will almost to the root. Then he looked up, his gaze met Will's, and shockwaves slammed through Will's blood.

One hand on the back of the sofa for balance, he raked the other hand through Koichi's damp hair. The sight of him like this—naked, kneeling, Will's cock in his mouth—was arresting. Addicting. Will knew he'd see this forever, imprinted on his brainwaves.

Koichi pulled off long enough to spit on his fingers, then swallowed Will down again. At first Will's blood-deprived mind wondered what Koichi was doing. Then Koichi groped for Will's hole and pushed a slim finger inside him. That clever fingertip hit his gland, again and again, and Will came with such force that his vision grayed at the edges.

Koichi swallowed, rubbing Will's thigh with the hand not still fingering his ass. When Will was on the verge of saying *enough*, Koichi pulled his finger carefully out of Will's body and sat back on the sofa, grinning. "Well. That was fun."

"I'll say." Will grinned back. He felt light, loopy, and a little bit silly. "I guess it would be wrong to just stay here and fuck all the time, huh?"

"Probably. Though it's awfully damn tempting." Koichi's smile faded as he studied the wreck of his living room. "For a little while I almost forgot what happened."

The sadness in Koichi's face hurt Will's heart. He sat, slid sideways, and wrapped both arms around Koichi's shoulders. "You're not alone. I'm gonna help you."

Koichi leaned into his embrace with a soft sigh. "You have no idea how much that means to me. Thank you."

"I'm glad I can help out." Will traced a thumb over the graceful arch of Koichi's collarbone. "Can I ask you something?"

"Sure." Koichi twisted his head to gaze at Will with curious eyes. "What is it?"

Now that it came to it, Will was nervous about bringing up the subject of moving in. But he made himself do it, because whoever had ransacked Koichi's house might come back. Which meant Koichi was in danger. "Is the offer to stay with you still open?"

Surprise, desire, happiness, and a hint of hesitation chased each other across Koichi's features. He blinked. "Of course it is. Do you want to come stay with me? Because that would be totally cool." A sweet smile curved his lips. "I don't mind saying, I like having you around."

If Will had still harbored any doubts, that would've erased them. He nuzzled Koichi's neck. "I like being around you too."

He didn't mention the part where he intended to protect Koichi from whoever might want to hurt him. But it was there, front and center. Will wasn't sure exactly what he felt for Koichi, but he knew they were friends, at least. Friends with the hots for each other, obviously. How far beyond that it went, he didn't yet know. But it didn't matter. Whatever he and Koichi were to each other, he intended to keep him safe.

Koichi sat back. "Well. I guess we better start cleaning up." He looked around and wrinkled his nose. "Ugh."

Will took his hand and squeezed. "You want to start in here?"

"Might as well, I guess." Koichi reached down, grabbed Will's wadded-up shorts, and tossed them at him. "Get dressed first, though. There will be no naked housecleaning in here."

"Damn. I was looking forward to you bending over with no pants on."

Koichi laughed. "Maybe another time, big guy." He kicked aside debris, gathered his clothes, stood, and flipped his T-shirt right side out. "Come on. I want to get some work out of you before you change your mind."

His tone teased, but Will heard real fear behind it. Setting his shorts on the couch, he rose and pulled Koichi close. Koichi stared up at him, serious and questioning, and Will held his gaze. "I'm not changing my mind. Okay?"

For a second Koichi didn't answer. Just stood there, studying Will's face with a slow, solemn look, as if trying to decide if he really meant it. Unsure of what to do, Will tried to tell him without words that he did. He was here to help. Whatever else might happen between them, whatever they might become to each other, he was Koichi's friend, and he would always have his back.

Finally, Koichi nodded. "Okay." He grasped Will's hand, his sunny smile coming back. "Let's get busy, then."

They pulled on their clothes, then started sorting through the mess. Will watched Koichi as they worked, and wondered what he was thinking.

The break-in made Koichi uneasy. Which was only natural. And he was pissed off that someone had taken his PlayStation. But he didn't truly worry, in his heart of hearts, until he realized Grammy's perfume bottle was missing.

Her mother had bought it in Paris back in the 1920s, part of a five-piece set. It was exquisite, small and round with delicate carvings in the translucent amber glass, still holding a faint whiff of some rare French fragrance. He knew it was worth a lot to the right collector, but he'd never been interested. To him, that tiny bit of etched glass spoke of his history. His *family*. Losing it to theft infuriated him. Not least because he shouldn't have let it happen.

"I'm going to strangle them with their own intestines," he told Will, calmly, because it was nothing but the truth. "I'm going to find them, cut them open with rusty scissors, wrap their guts around their greedy little throats, and *fucking. Strangle* them."

"I know." Will patted him on the shoulder really hard, which effectively pushed him into the desk chair in his home office. He wanted to jump right up again, glare and rant and say he *really meant it*, damn it, but Will started massaging his shoulders, thumbs digging into the knots of tension he hadn't realized were there until now, and he relaxed almost in spite of himself. "I'll help you, T. I swear. Later. First, we have to tell the police so they can figure out who did it, and why, and find them." He leaned over and planted a soft kiss on Koichi's cheek. "And you need to settle down before you have a stroke."

Koichi sighed, partly from frustration, and partly because Will was right. "Grammy gave me that bottle, Will. It was her mother's. It's a fucking *heirloom*, and I lost it."

"What?" The sweet pressure of the shoulder massage stopped. Will walked around and stood in front of Koichi, practically crackling with righteous indignation. "You didn't *lose* it, you idiot. Some jackass *stole* it. Not the same thing." He leaned closer, those beautiful brown eyes narrowing. "You do realize that, right?"

He did. Technically. Still . . . He bit his lip.

Will threw his hands in the air. "Oh my God. Really?"

"Okay, so I have problems with guilt." Angry and confused and feeling no less irrationally responsible than before, Koichi jumped to his feet and stomped to the other side of the room, where he could stand with his arms crossed and feel protected from Will's common sense and reasonableness. "I know it's stupid, all right? I know that. But I can't help it."

Sighing, Will pinched the bridge of his nose. "No offense or anything, but that's the flakiest thing I've ever heard."

That hurt a little, but Koichi wasn't about to let on. He did his best smirk-and-eyebrow-lift. "My last boyfriend said I was flaky too, only he called it 'complex and layered.'"

Will glowered. "That's not funny."

"I wasn't trying to be funny." Which wasn't really a lie. Tristan *had* called him complex and layered, which in Tristan-ese meant flaky. It didn't sting any less now than it had then. "I prefer my insults straight up rather than hidden inside fake compliments."

"Jesus Christ." Will covered his face with both hands. "Why are you being so defensive?"

Koichi started to answer, and realized he *had* no answer. He dropped his arms to his side. "Honestly? I don't even know. I just get that way sometimes. It's ridiculous. I get . . ."

Crazy. Hysterical. Bad as a fucking girl. Nearly three years after their break-up, Tristan's parting words still had the power to form a lump of fury, shame, and humiliation in his gut. If Tristan hadn't been in the process of leaving him, Koichi would've cut him loose then and there. And still, even knowing that Tristan was the one who'd done all the hurting and putting-down in their relationship, Koichi felt he should've seen the misogynist bully behind the handsome face. He should've known not to get involved. It was *his fault* all along, even though it wasn't.

"Koichi?"

He blinked. Will was watching him with concern. He forced a smile. "Sorry. I was thinking of a relationship that ended badly."

Realization flowed over Will's features. "Flaky guy."

The blood rushed into Koichi's face. "Maybe."

"Maybe, my butt." Will shook his head, his mouth tight and his hands on his hips in a way that reminded Koichi of his mom when she was frustrated with her brood. "Christ. Okay. Is there anything else missing?"

Koichi's stomach unknotted a little. He really didn't want to keep talking—or arguing—about his weird guilt complexes and personality flaws. "I haven't found anything yet. But there's still a lot to sort through. I'm not calling Beauchamp until I've gone through the whole place, just in case."

"Yeah. That makes sense." Will took a deep breath and blew it out. "Well. Back to work, then."

"Back to work." Koichi brushed past Will, heading for the hall and the upstairs rooms they hadn't touched yet.

All the way up the stairs, he felt Will's gaze on the back of his neck.

In the end, he found a few other things missing: the DVR player and plasma-screen TV from his bedroom, the speakers from the extra bedroom he used as a library now—though not the rest of his high-end sound system, he noticed—and, weirdly, an old hand-penned journal he'd found in the attic as a child, when he and Kimmy had been poking around looking for treasure. It was written in French, which he couldn't read, so he had no idea what was in it, but he'd kept it because he'd thought it was cool.

Evidently someone else had agreed so much that they'd stolen it.

"It bugs me," he told Will as the two of them reshelved his books. "Not so much because the journal's gone, but because that's what they took. You know? I mean, who takes something like that, unless they already know something about it?"

"I see your point." Will eased a ragged paperback copy of *Dune* into its place, then sat cross-legged on the floor, looking thoughtful. "But why would an expert on old French journals rob your house? If they knew you had it and they wanted it, why wouldn't they just ask if they could buy it?"

"Same reason other people steal shit. 'Cause they don't want to pay for it." Koichi sat beside Will, feeling nervous and defeated. "I gotta be honest, this is freaking me out a little. I can't help feeling like all the mess and the missing TVs and stuff are just a distraction."

Will cast him a sharp glance. "You think they were really after the journal or the perfume bottle all along."

It wasn't a question. Maybe this was a strange time for warm fuzzies, but Koichi sort of liked how Will's thoughts were so in sync with his own.

He nodded. "I think they might've stolen the other stuff and wrecked the place to cover up what they were really after and make it look like a normal robbery."

Will's expression turned grave. "We need to figure out who might've known those things were worth money."

"That's just it, though. No one would have known the perfume bottle even existed, other than our family. Grammy gave each of her grandkids one bottle out of her set of five. We have them, but we don't exactly advertise."

"And the journal?"

Koichi shrugged. "I found it in this house ages ago, when me and Kimmy were kids and we were playing in the attic. I never even told anyone but her and Grammy. I asked Grammy if I could keep it and she said I could. She said she didn't know where it came from, and she didn't want it. And who knows if it's even worth a damn dime?"

"It must be, or they wouldn't have stolen it."

"Good point."

Will's brows drew together. He sucked on his bottom lip, his eyes unfocused. "So what we have here, aside from the missing electronics, is a stolen perfume bottle and a stolen journal written in French, neither of which anyone outside your family ought to know you had, and only one of which is worth anything as far as you know. Right?"

"That's about the size of it." Koichi turned in a circle, surveying his newly cleaned library. It gave him the creeps to imagine some stranger in here pawing through his things. "You know, this whole mystery business isn't nearly as awesome as I used to think it would be when I was a kid."

Will laughed. "Funny how things always turn out like that, huh?"

"Yeah." With a deep sigh, Koichi planted himself on the floor beside Will. "Well, there's one bright spot."

"What's that?"

"Now I have an excuse to use the restricted section of the library."

"Uh." Will cut him a look suggesting he'd gone off his meds. "That's not really a thing."

"It is here." Koichi grinned. He loved telling people Duchene's public library was like a real-life Hogwarts. Sort of. "The public library has a historical-documents section that requires ID, signature, and permission of the librarian to access, because some of the books, journals, and other documents in there are so old and fragile. They want a paper trail of who's accessed what and why."

"I see." Will watched him with equal parts amusement and intrigue in his dark eyes and wry smile. "And you want to go to the restricted section to try to learn about your mysterious journal?"

"Exactly. If I can figure out what it is and how it ended up at my house, maybe I can figure out who might've stolen it, and what they'd want with it."

He didn't spell out the rest of his reasoning, but Will picked up on it anyway. "Because even if they didn't come here specifically for that journal, they stole it for a reason. And if they think you have other similar valuables, they might be back looking for them."

Neither of them voiced Koichi's number one fear: that whoever had done this might deliberately hurt him—or worse, his family—in the mistaken belief that he knew where to find more treasure. He didn't. Hadn't known the journal was worth anything other than as a curiosity. But he doubted the truth mattered to greedy, thieving thugs.

Shutting his eyes, he leaned against Will's shoulder. Will's strength felt good. Comforting. Calming. Koichi had always had a fertile imagination. He knew that. He wanted to believe that was what made him think he was a target. But his gut told him this time it wasn't in his mind.

Will wrapped an arm around him and kissed his hair. "You okay?"

Opening his eyes, he tilted his head and smiled at Will. "I'm fine."

CHAPTER 8

As soon as they'd finished cleaning up, Will went to the shop to gather the few personal belongings he'd brought with him from Texas, then came straight back to Koichi's place in spite of Koichi's objections.

"You should've stayed and opened the shop," Koichi told him. "You could've gotten a few hours of business. It's better than nothing."

He shook his head. "I've already been closed most of the day. Another three or four hours isn't going to make that much difference."

Koichi pursed his lips. "It's a whole day of lost business. That's not good."

"It's no big deal. Your sister hung a sign on my door saying I'm closed for the day, and she's even trying to catch anyone who looks like a potential customer so she can try to answer any questions they might have. It's fine."

"But, Will—"

"Koichi. Hush." Setting his bag on the living room floor, he cupped Koichi's worried, stubborn face between his hands and kissed him, partly to shut him up and partly because kissing him felt so damn good and Will still couldn't quite believe he was allowed to do it. "It's already obvious to me that most of my income's going to come from glamping trips, not equipment sales from the shop. And the trips are mostly being booked online. So you can stop worrying now, all right?"

The frown line between Koichi's eyes eased a bit, but didn't go away entirely. "I will if you will."

It was a fair point. Except that Will had far more reason to worry about Koichi than the other way around. "I'll worry about you a lot less now that I'm here to help watch out for you."

Koichi rolled his eyes. "Christ almighty. How alpha dog can you get? Do I look like a damsel in distress to you?"

"Not even remotely." Will flashed his best rakish grin, because he didn't want Koichi to see the part of him that really did want to bristle and growl and *protect* like a goddamn animal. "Humor me, will you? I need my masculinity validated."

Koichi sighed, the very picture of put-out-ed-ness. "That's pathetic, Will. Seriously."

"Believe me, I know." He kissed Koichi again, a slower, softer kiss that got him a happy little hum as a reward. "Why don't you go put your feet up? I'll cook dinner."

Koichi's hands tightened on his shoulders. "You don't need to do that."

"I know. In case you didn't notice, I love to cook. And now I have access to a real kitchen." He gave Koichi a playful shove. "Go sit."

Koichi cracked his knuckles, watching Will with a curious glint in his eyes. "Actually, I'd like to help. If it's okay with you, that is. I've always wanted to learn how to cook better."

Will raised his eyebrows. Koichi blushed and stared at the floor, and Will's heart melted. He took Koichi's hand. "In that case, let's go play in the kitchen."

Koichi's face lit up with a purely joyful smile, and Will knew that was it. He was lost.

The next day was, as Kimmy put it later, *fucking insane.* Will was run off his feet from the time he unlocked his shop doors to the time he closed an hour late, having herded out the lingering shoppers with Kimmy's help and pulled down the shades in their unhappy faces.

He flopped onto the floor, exhausted and stunned at the amount of business he'd done. "Oh my God. I wish I knew if it was going to be like this every day, 'cause if it is, I might have to hire some help."

"Wish I could tell you, but I can't. It's a fickle business." Kimmy settled on the floor beside him, her legs folded beneath her. "If you want to know what I think, though, I think you'd do well to hire somebody. I mean, even if every day isn't like today, you're still gonna have busy times, and you're gonna need time off. Plus you'll need to have downtime to manage the books and stuff."

That was a good point. One he hadn't thought of. "You're right." He sat up, hugging his knees to his chest. "Any idea where I should start?"

"The usual online spots, of course. And I'd place an ad in the Mobile *Press-Register*. It'll run in their print and online papers, so a shitload of prospective employees will see it. People who know the local area, which is important if you want someone to help you out with your expeditions." She cast him a sidelong glance. "Listen, I know you didn't ask, but I think it would be a good idea if you included catering from local businesses on your expeditions. Like, maybe even places here in the mall. You could boost each other's business, you know?"

The idea hadn't even occurred to him, but it was a good one. He reached out and pulled her into an impulsive hug. "Oh man, that's great. You're so smart. Thanks."

"My pleasure." She sat back, grinning. "I like sharing with people who appreciate my business acumen."

"Well, I definitely do."

The sound of his screen door in back squealing open distracted him from asking her for any further details.

"Hey!" Koichi called from the storeroom. "Where y'all at?"

Will twisted toward his voice like a sunflower following the light. "We're up front. C'mon in."

A moment later Koichi strolled into the shop, looking as tired as Will felt. He sat on the floor, leaned in, and collected a swift but firm kiss. "What a day. I'm beat."

Will started to respond, but Kimmy cut him off. "Hang on a sec. When did this happen?"

Will blinked at her in false innocence, though he figured he knew what she meant. "What?"

"Don't give me that. *This*." She circled her finger in the air, drawing an imaginary line around him and Koichi. "When did y'all hook up?"

He looked at Koichi, who widened his eyes in silent pleading. Will shook his head. Nope. Kimmy was Koichi's sister. It was his job to explain.

Koichi's shoulders slumped for a second, but he rallied, straightened his spine, and faced his twin. "When we were out in the swamp. Then again at my house when he was helping me clean up. Then he moved in last night, and we did this thing where—"

"Yeah, I don't want to know." She reached out and grasped her brother's hands in hers. "Look, all kidding aside, I'm glad. You're good for each other. You make each other happy. And that makes *me* happy." She smiled, showing dimples. "It's late, and I know for a fact we all missed lunch. Why don't we go get something to eat? My treat."

Until that moment, Will hadn't considered that he'd skipped a meal. But the reminder made his stomach knot and grumble. "I could definitely eat. I can pay my own way, though."

She *pfft*ed. "I'm aware, He-Man. But I'm paying this time." She bounced to her feet like she hadn't been standing on them for going on twelve hours. "Come on. Oyster Shack's still open. Let's go."

He stood and pulled Koichi up with him, and they followed Kimmy out the back door, holding hands. It felt good, Will decided, to have someone to hold hands with.

In spite of being the only restaurant for miles around open after nine, Oyster Shack wasn't particularly crowded. Week nights in April didn't tend to draw the tourists. The three of them were seated after only a short wait, and sat sipping tea and eating fried pickles while they waited for the Shack's famous oyster po'boys to arrive.

"So." Kimmy dipped a pickle slice in ranch sauce and took a bite. "What did you find out about the break-in at your house, T? Was anything else missing?"

Will gaped. "You mean you haven't told her yet?"

"There hasn't been time!" Koichi stabbed his straw into his tea like it had done him wrong. "We've had customers in the shop all day. I didn't want to talk about it in front of them."

Kimmy covered her brother's hand with her own. "Relax. Nobody blames you for that. But now we have some time, and I'm dying to hear about it."

Will listened without interrupting while Koichi gave the sex-free version of how they'd slogged through the mess and found out about the missing perfume bottle and journal. Listening to Koichi retell the story, he felt more certain than ever that this hadn't been a random burglary. Koichi had been deliberately targeted, either for the perfume bottle, the journal, or something else the thieves had expected to find in the house.

A sudden realization sent a hard chill down Will's spine. "Hang on," he said, interrupting something Kimmy was saying. "Did they know you were gone? Or did they plan on robbing your place while you were home?"

The twins fell silent, each staring at Will with the same alarm that sank icy claws into his soul. If whoever had hit the place had known Koichi would be gone, that meant they were watching him. But if they'd been prepared to go in thinking he'd be at home, did that mean they were willing to deliberately hurt him to get what they wanted?

Will didn't much like either scenario.

Koichi fidgeted in his seat. "Okay, let's think about this. There's no way anybody knew about that stupid journal, and I don't think it's likely to be worth much anyway. And I think Will's right that your average TV thief wouldn't have bothered trashing the place. So they must've been after the bottle."

Kimmy's expression turned grave. "I hate to even think it, but you're probably right."

Koichi fished a thin, crispy pickle slice from the middle of the pile and popped it into his mouth. "What bugs me is, how does whoever did this know I even had that bottle? I mean, any way you look at it, it's bad, 'cause it means they must've been watching me for a while now. At least since the fire, anyway. Asking questions and stuff. It's seriously creepy."

"Oh my God." Kimmy froze with a ranch-dripping pickle in her hand and pure horror on her face. "Koichi, we need to call the girls."

The same horror flooded Koichi's face and widened his eyes. "Shit. You're right."

Confused, Will glanced from one to the other. "The girls?"

"Our sisters," Kimmy said. "Bonnie, Lyric, and Akiri. They each have their own perfume bottle. And so do I, but I locked mine in my safe-deposit box this morning. The robbery at your place spooked the shit out of me."

Will nodded. "I don't know if these people would know about the other bottles, but if they knew about yours, they might know it's part of a set. Better safe than sorry."

He plucked a fried pickle from the top of the heap and frowned at it. The twins had sworn fried pickles were better than sex, but it didn't look that great to him. Deciding what the hell, he dunked it in ranch and bit into it. Flavor exploded over his tongue, and he closed his eyes in bliss. "Oh, wow. That is fantastic." He ate the rest with a happy little moan.

"Told you." Koichi's voice was teasing and a little smug. When Will opened his eyes, Koichi's smile matched his tone. "You should learn how to make 'em for your trips."

It was a good idea. Will opened his mouth to agree.

Kimmy interrupted before he got a word out. "Oh shit. The picture." She grasped Koichi's wrist hard in one hand, her eyes alight with the fever of discovery. "The *picture!*"

For a second, Koichi looked as clueless as Will felt. Then his face went slack and pallid. "We had a picture in our old shop of Kimmy, Grammy, and me," he explained before Will could ask. "It was the three of us in front of the old glass-front cabinet in my office at home. It was her office before she moved out." He grabbed Will's hand and clung. "In the picture, the whole set of perfume bottles was lined up on the shelf in the cabinet behind us. You could see it clear as day."

The implications hit Will just as it had the twins. "So whoever hit the old shop and burned it could've seen that picture, figured out where it was taken, and known where to look for the bottles."

Kimmy nodded. "And they only found the one. So they might not be done with us yet."

Dread curled tight in the pit of Will's stomach. Koichi looked sick. Will slipped an arm around his waist, which got him a halfhearted smile.

"I'll call Beauchamp tonight," Koichi said. "He needs to put a guard on the girls. I don't want them or their families to get hurt."

In the following silence, the waitress arrived with their sandwiches. While she set out plates piled with overstuffed po'boys, coleslaw, and french fries, the three of them stared at each other with the same wordless questions in their eyes: What now? How long would they spend looking over their shoulders? Would they ever feel safe again?

Will didn't have any answers. And he wasn't sure how to feel about the fact that he'd automatically included himself.

CHAPTER 9

After a month and change with no further break-ins, Kimmy started to relax and the girls told Beauchamp to cancel the patrols hanging around their houses. Even Will had stopped frowning at everybody like they might be secret ax murderers.

Koichi, however, remained nervous. He wasn't sure why. Nothing out of the ordinary had happened. He hadn't caught any sinister strangers skulking around his house or following him on his errands. He just couldn't shake the sensation of being watched. Of unfriendly eyes trained on him. It was stupid and he knew it, but his logic-brain couldn't seem to talk his instinct-brain out of it. The upshot being, he was jumpy as a damn Chihuahua all the time lately.

At least he'd found a distraction. Not that it made him any less nervous, really, but it gave him a channel for it.

The library was mostly deserted, as usual on a Sunday afternoon. He grinned at the librarian as he approached the desk. "Hey, Georgia. How's it going?"

"Can't complain." She smiled back, producing fine lines around her eyes and mouth. "You headed to the historical section again?"

"Yep. I think I'm closing in."

He'd asked her about the journal soon after it was stolen, since she was an expert on local history, but she knew nothing specific or rumored about it. So he'd turned to the old records in the restricted section. "Closing in" might be an exaggeration, but it wasn't a lie. He'd pretty much decided it wasn't any older than 1900, anyway. Which was something, right?

While he signed the register for the historical-documents section, she rose and skirted the desk, her library badge in hand. He followed her to the far side of the bright little building and waited while she held her badge up to the card reader. The light on the lock went from red to green. Georgia opened the door, and they both went in.

Koichi drew a deep breath. The room smelled like old paper, dry and slightly musty. The smell of childhood, of the books that had been his refuge when the world was too hard.

Sometimes Will got impatient with him for coming here all the time on his days off. Not that he actually said so, but Koichi could tell. He thought maybe Will would understand if he came here and caught the scent of happy memories.

"Which years will you be checking today?" Georgia asked, booting up the computer terminal.

Koichi considered. "1890 through 1910."

She arched an eyebrow at him, but went to see what they had from those years. It wasn't a completely random selection. He'd gotten tired of going in chronological order almost immediately and had started jumping around. Last week he'd found a single intriguing mention in a local paper from 1927 about a French jewel thief who'd supposedly vanished from Duchene in the early 1900s, leaving behind a fortune in stolen jewels. It wasn't much—only a couple of sentences out of a long interview with a woman influential in local society at the time—but it was such a colorful tale, he wondered why it hadn't been passed down as part of the local folklore. It seemed reasonable to find out more about it. Specifically, whether or not this French thief might have kept a journal.

"All right, my dear." Georgia rose from the rolling chair and gestured for him to sit. "Here's the list of what we have. It's not very much, I'm sorry to say, but I'll pull whatever you'd like to look at."

Koichi settled into the chair and studied the index. She was right, there wasn't a lot to choose from. "Um. Let's see. Let me look at the police records first. Arrest records and calls, I guess. Then I'll check the gossip columns."

"There won't be any call records from that time period, since this area didn't have any phones then. But I can get you the arrest records and gossip columns."

"Oh. Okay, cool." He laughed. "Hard to imagine a time when there weren't any phones."

Shaking her head, Georgia went into the stacks to look for the volumes he needed. "I'm assuming there's some sort of logic behind this."

"Kind of." He shrugged, though she couldn't see him. "I'm not sure it would make sense to anyone but me, but yeah, there's a plan."

"Well, as long as it makes sense to you." She emerged from between the shelves, carrying three thick hardbound volumes. "You won't be surprised to learn that we have one volume of arrest records, and two volumes of gossip columns from the years you're looking at today." She plunked the books down on the table. "Happy reading, Koichi. No gloves or oversight necessary today. These are all photocopies. Let me know if you need me."

"Will do." He grasped her hand and gave it a squeeze. "Thanks, Georgia. You're the best."

"If only everyone thought so."

He laughed, and she patted his back on her way out. Alone, he settled in to skim through the pages of police reports and gossip.

Almost three hours later, he found the clue he'd been looking for in a second-rate rag called *True Crime of Southern Alabama*. An issue from March of 1904 told the story—heavily embellished with purple prose and lurid illustrations—of a Frenchman called Severin Lamar who'd arrived from New York in late summer 1900 and proceeded to spread shock and scandal throughout the tiny settlement of Duchene. He'd spent outlandish amounts of money—inherited, said some; ill-gotten, said others—all over the area, then disappeared without a trace in the winter of 1902. The community still had been talking about it at the time of the *True Crime* story over a year later, though the tale evidently hadn't survived for long after that.

Two things stood out to Koichi. First, rumor at the time had it that the man had been lost in Hunter's Bog. Second, during his time in Duchene he'd supposedly lived in a rented room at the Duchene Guest House, at 47 Cotton Street.

Koichi didn't recognize the name of the house, but he recognized the address. He lived there.

When Koichi got home that evening, he had to knock on his own back door with his foot because his hands were full. "Will! Let me in."

Will opened the door a few seconds later, stood aside, and let him pass. "Wow. What's all that?"

"Copies and dinner." Koichi set the box full of photocopies on the kitchen table, handed Will the bag full of Krystal burgers and fries, and stood on tiptoe to plant a kiss on his mouth. "I think I finally found the origin story of my journal."

"Oh, really? That's great."

Koichi headed to the cabinet to grab paper plates and napkins, turning his back so Will wouldn't see the disappointment he couldn't quite hide. Part of him appreciated that Will bothered to pretend to share his enthusiasm for learning about the journal. Another part wished like hell it *wasn't* a pretense. But no relationship was perfect, and no couple shared every interest. That sort of shit was nothing but a fantasy. They got along great, they had a lot in common, and the sex was phenomenal. All he had to do now was not overthink it like he usually did. Not withdraw. Not back off from a good thing because he was scared.

Don't fuck this up just because it's not perfect.

Will's arms around his waist startled him. He relaxed into the embrace that was becoming wonderfully, alarmingly familiar. "Hey, you know I'm always happy to be molested. But the food's gonna get cold."

Will *hmm*ed into his neck. "I really am happy for you, you know. Just because I'm not so into the mystery doesn't mean I don't care."

A sweet ache lodged deep in Koichi's chest. He laid his hands over Will's. Rubbed his cheek against Will's stubbly one. "I know," he said, though that wasn't entirely true. "And believe me, I appreciate your putting up with my weird obsession. Not everybody would."

He'd tried for a teasing tone, but Will didn't laugh. "Anybody who cared about you would."

And there it was. *I care about you.* Not that it was a news flash or anything. They'd been friends from day one, and now they were . . . more than that. Obviously they cared about each other. Still, having it out there so baldly felt a little too open. Too raw.

Back up, said the inner Koichi who had never felt comfortable being close to anyone other than his twin. *Close off. Clam up. Pill bug. Protect, protect, protect.*

No, argued the new Koichi, the one who'd promised himself he'd try. *Let it happen.*

Gathering all his courage, Koichi turned in Will's arms and peered up into his solemn dark eyes. "Me too. That is, I care. About you. And your stuff. That is, the stuff you like."

Christ almighty. Koichi cringed. No one had ever accused him of eloquence, but this was a new low.

Judging by the smile that lit Will's face, he may as well have recited a Shakespearean sonnet. Will laid his hands on Koichi's cheeks. "I know you do. Thank you for saying that." He bent and kissed Koichi's lips.

It was restrained, as kisses went. Light, quick, and close-mouthed, affectionate rather than passionate. But the touch zinged along Koichi's nerve endings like an electric charge. A quiet, idle part of his mind wondered what it meant that even the most innocent kiss from Will affected him so strongly.

Will drew back, still smiling. "Guess what I did today?"

"Robbed a bank?" Koichi turned and reached for the paper plates, giving Will his best serious face over his shoulder. "No, you wouldn't do that. Oh, I know, you invented a hover car. Finally, I get the future my childhood promised me."

Shaking his head, Will took the plates Koichi handed him and set them on the table. "You and Kimmy must've given your parents hell."

"We did our best." Koichi went to the fridge for ketchup and a couple of the coconut waters Will had gotten him to like over the past few weeks. "I guess that means no hover cars."

"Sorry, no." Will loaded a plate with fries and four Krystal burgers and handed it to Koichi, along with a wide grin. "But I *did* ask Joanie if she wanted to go full-time at the shop. And she said yes."

It was fabulous news. Will had hired Joanie three weeks earlier to work part-time, and she'd been a real godsend. Full-time for her meant more downtime for Will.

"Well, *finally*." Koichi cracked open his can of coconut water and held it up. "Here's to more days off."

"Amen to that. Cheers."

They clinked cans and drank. For a while they ate in comfortable silence. Koichi studied Will's face on the sly in between ketchup-dredged fries and bites of miniature burgers. Will seemed as content as he'd been ever since moving in. He laughed a lot, and smiled more often than not. But his eyes were oceans, hiding dark secrets beneath their surface sparkle. Koichi often wondered what those secrets were, and how much they would eventually hurt him.

Don't borrow trouble, Kimmy had told him the other day, even though he hadn't said a word to her about his worries and fears. She knew him well enough to read him like a damn billboard. *He's obviously happy with you. You're happy with a man for the first time in your nitpicky life. Enjoy it. Don't sabotage it by inventing problems where there aren't any.*

She was right. His logic-brain agreed with her. Just this once, he should ignore the cynical (sensible?) part of him that didn't believe anything this good could last. Just because he'd never had a relationship that hadn't ended badly didn't mean it couldn't happen.

Will swallowed a mouthful of fries and peered at him with a frown. "What're you thinking about? You look so serious."

"Nothing much." It was only a tiny lie. Necessary, because how would he explain his stupid anxieties to anyone, especially Will? He plastered on a well-practiced grin. "Hey, we haven't been out to the bog in a while by ourselves. You wanna go? Joanie could cover the shop for you."

Will's eyes narrowed. Koichi held his breath. Will had gotten very good at reading him, and he didn't want to explain why he was changing the subject.

After a few seconds that felt like years, Will nodded and laughed. "That would actually be fantastic. I'll talk to Joanie and see when she can cover me." He reached across the table to grasp Koichi's hand. "It'll be nice to get out in the wild with you again."

All the reasons burned in his eyes. Pulse racing, Koichi shifted his grip to lace his fingers through Will's. "I can't wait."

Koichi was hiding something.

After the whole business with Anthony, Will knew when a man was keeping secrets from him. And Koichi definitely had secrets.

It hurt a little. But Will had already decided it was nothing to worry about. It *couldn't* be, because he couldn't face another Anthony situation. He couldn't deal with that again, even if his emotional investment this time wasn't quite the same. Therefore, whatever Koichi was keeping from him must be something small. Something personal. Something he had to work out for himself. *Not* something big and bad enough to make him run like Anthony had.

Maybe that was wishful thinking. It certainly wasn't any sort of logical reasoning. But Will had to believe it, or he'd unravel.

Working helped. Part of him almost wished Joanie hadn't agreed to full-time, even though it meant he'd actually get to keep the shop open more often while he took groups out on glamping expeditions. Not to mention having days off for a change. That was supposed to be a good thing.

She'd been dropping hints since her first week that she was perfectly capable of looking after the shop while he took a day off, so he decided on a test run. "You're in charge for the afternoon," he told her, trying to pretend he wasn't nervous about it. "I'm gonna go out and do some errands. I'll be back by around seven. Call my cell if you need me."

She nodded, dark eyes calm. "Everything'll be fine, Will. Don't worry."

"I'm not worried." Which was true, sort of. He wasn't worried about the shop, or her ability to manage things. He *was* worried about how he'd handle being at loose ends. His short to-do list wouldn't take up six hours. "So. Uh. See you later."

She laughed, putting a dimple in one brown cheek. Skirting the desk, she took his elbow and escorted him to the door. Her yellow skirt swirled around her calves. "Go *on*, you workaholic. Get out. Go see a movie or something."

A movie. Christ, he hadn't gone to the movies in *years*. "Maybe. Thanks, Joanie."

"Of course." Behind her, the shop phone rang. She made a shooing motion at him and went to answer it.

Resisting the urge to follow and see who it was, he pushed the door open and strode out into the steamy midday heat. Clouds loomed black and threatening on the horizon to the south. Thunder growled in the distance.

Will breathed in the thick scent of approaching rain. Maybe he'd head into Duchene and take a stroll through the park before the storm hit. In fact, maybe he wouldn't leave when it started raining. He had an umbrella in his truck, and he'd always found walking in the rain relaxing. It cleared his mind. Helped him think.

By the time he got to the surprisingly large green space nestled in the center of Duchene's colorful downtown area, the black cloud had caught up to him and the thunder had gone from a rumble to a *crack-boom* hot on the heels of the lightning. The trees thrashed in the wind. He parked, snatched the War Eagle umbrella Kimmy had loaned him from under the passenger seat, and ran for the shelter of the picturesque gazebo at the far end of the park. The first raindrops caught the backs of his legs as he bounded up the steps.

Will stood in the middle of the whitewashed wooden floor and watched the solid wall of falling water form puddles in the grass. The temperature must've dropped ten degrees with the clouds and the cool, damp breeze. He found the spot where he seemed the least likely to get drenched, and sat on the bench to watch the storm sweep through the town.

He peered through the gray curtain of rain at the shops and restaurants on either side of the park. A few people dashed from store to store, heads down against the deluge or huddled under umbrellas, but thanks to the weather he had the place mostly to himself. Already his mind felt calmer. More peaceful. He ought to pack a picnic lunch and bring Koichi here sometime. Maybe if they came here on a stormy afternoon, when they were cut off from the world by the thrum of rain on the gazebo's roof, Koichi would open up and tell Will what was bothering him.

Headlights swung around the corner behind him. A car's engine rumbled nearby, then cut off. Curious about who besides him would be coming to the park in the rain, he turned to look. A newer model Mercedes was parked in the last space in the row. Will could just make out two shadowy figures in the front seat.

Will's curiosity rose higher every second the mystery people sat in the car. What were they doing in there? Watching the rain, like he was? Doing a drug deal? Jesus, maybe these were the guys who'd robbed Koichi's house and burned down his shop. Who knew what else they'd done.

Stop it. They're probably just having a private talk.

He chuckled. People-watching was fine, but his habit of inventing outlandish stories for random strangers tended to get out of hand.

The passenger side door of the Mercedes opened. A person in a dark-blue hooded raincoat got out, shut the door, and started across the end of the park, head down and hands in the coat's pockets.

A man, Will thought, watching the figure stride away. Of course he had no way of knowing for sure, but there was something male about the set of the shoulders and the swing of the narrow hips. He shifted on the bench to watch, letting his imagination roam free for now. Why not? There was no harm. It wasn't like the stranger knew what he was thinking.

To his surprise, the man pulled a set of keys out of his pocket and unlocked a rust-spotted white pickup on the other side of the park. Will leaned on the railing and squinted, trying to see better. Why was this person getting out of one car and into another one? That was sort of suspicious, wasn't it?

Well, no, not necessarily. There were all sorts of perfectly innocuous reasons for a guy to leave his truck in a central location and ride somewhere with someone else, then come back. Hell, Will had done the same thing, more than once.

"Stop being stupid," he told himself, out loud so he'd be more likely to listen. Maybe he should head on out and start his errands. Clearly free time was bad for his brain.

He rose, umbrella in hand. He cast one last glance toward the mysterious stranger.

The man was standing beside the battered old truck, staring straight at Will.

Goose bumps rose on Will's arms. Why was that man staring at him? Had he seen Will watching him? Christ, what if this stranger actually *was* involved in something illegal, and he thought Will knew about it?

Cold fear spread through his blood like poison. Heart in his throat, he turned away, raised his umbrella, and descended the gazebo steps into the lessening storm. Once he'd reached his truck and locked himself safely inside, he peered through the rain to the other side of the park.

The rusty white pickup was gone.

CHAPTER 10

Koichi had heard Will's stories about random strangers before. But this was a whole level up.

"Let me see if I understand this." He planted his elbows on the wooden table of the Oyster Shack, where he and Will had gone to grab dinner, and peered at Will through narrowed eyes. "You were watching this guy walk across the park, and making up your usual horse shit about what he might be up to. And you're saying that when you stood up to leave, he stopped and *stared* at you. Is that right?"

Will nodded, serious as a stroke. "I know it doesn't sound like much. But he looked at me like he had reasons for not wanting to be watched."

"I thought you said he was too far away for you to see his face."

"Yeah, but I didn't need to. He stopped what he was doing and stood perfectly still, with his head turned toward me." Will rubbed his arms like he was cold. "He was staring at me. I could *feel* it. And I don't mind telling you, it scared me a little."

That was a sobering thought. Will might have an active imagination, but he didn't scare easily. Still, Koichi couldn't see any logical reason to be afraid.

"He probably just thought you were hot." That got him the sweet, childlike laugh he'd learned to cherish over the past month. Smiling, he touched Will's hand. "Not that I blame him. But he better not be moving in on my territory. Just sayin'."

Will's eyes went hooded and hot, like they always did when Koichi's alpha streak turned him on. "Too bad for him if he tried, 'cause I'm not interested."

"Good."

They stared at each other across the table. All around them, people talked and laughed and ate their seafood like they didn't feel the sexual tension crackling between Will and Koichi. To be fair, they probably didn't. No reason they should, really. But at times like this, when he had to talk himself out of jumping on Will and molesting him and damn the crowd, he marveled that no one else noticed.

The waiter chose that moment to bring their order of fried crab claws. Which was just as well. Koichi had never felt unsafe here—"live and let live" was the prevailing philosophy—but he didn't want to push his luck by kissing his lover in public.

He dipped a plump crab claw in cocktail sauce and stripped the tender meat off the cartilage with his teeth. "So, how'd it go with Joanie flying solo today?"

"Terrific. She outsold me by probably thirty percent." Will dropped the shell of his second claw on the plate and took a swallow of beer. "I should concentrate on the glamping part and leave the retail part to her. She's better at it than me."

Koichi laughed. "She has a talent for making people think it was *their* idea to buy all that stuff."

"This is true." Will leaned forward, his face alight with a sudden excitement. "So what about that camping trip we were talking about? We could do it tomorrow night if you want. If Kimmy's okay with you being gone, that is."

Oh, hell yeah. Koichi grinned. "She's already been warned that I'm running away to the bog sometime this weekend. Bonnie said she could come help out at the shop, so it's all good."

Will grinned back. "In that case, why don't we get an early start? We can leave right after lunch. Joanie doesn't start full-time until next week, but she's working tomorrow already, so I'm covered."

"Sounds perfect to me."

"Great. It's a date, then."

They sealed the deal by clinking their beer glasses together. Koichi ate another perfectly cooked crab claw. He couldn't remember when he'd felt this happy. If a magic genie popped into being right now and told him he could change one thing in his life by wishing it, he honestly wouldn't be able to think of a single thing.

Well. Maybe one. He'd banish the melancholy that hid behind Will's smile and dragged his spirit down when it ought to fly.

Acting on impulse, Koichi took Will's hand firmly in his. "You make me incredibly happy," he said, softly, for Will's ears only. "I know I'm not the most demonstrative person in the world. But I wanted you to know that."

The startled look on Will's face melted into a joy so pure Koichi's throat went tight. "You don't know how much that means to me. Thank you." Will's voice was hoarse and choked. His fingers held Koichi's in a hard grip. "And the feeling's mutual, by the way. In case you wondered."

Koichi laughed, and so did Will. A couple of the nearby patrons frowned at them, but that was all right because *they* were all right. Maybe they had a few things to work out, but what couple didn't?

It's gonna be okay, said the inner Koichi, the one who was trying. *We're gonna be okay.*

He almost believed himself.

Ever since that first adventure in Hunter's Bog, standard gear for Koichi and Will's solo trips had included condoms and lube.

Thank God.

"I. Love. Your. Ass," Koichi panted, slamming into Will's gorgeous butt with each word. The heat and tightness came right through the thin latex, and Christ almighty, it was better than *anything*. "Fucking perfect."

Will moaned and shoved himself backward, one hand planted on the cypress tree and the other busy between his legs.

That would not do.

Talking was getting difficult, but Koichi managed one more word—"Wait."

Will, bless him, knew what that meant. He shot Koichi a frantic look over his shoulder, but he stopped getting himself off and put his jerk-off hand on the tree beside his bracing-himself hand.

A hard shudder ran down Koichi's spine. He loved it when Will *minded* him like that. God only knew no one else ever had.

Will's unhesitating obedience plus the warm, living grip of his body coiled the pleasure hard and tight in Koichi's balls. He got a good grip on Will's hips and pounded into him with all his strength, until his orgasm exploded like an A-bomb, shooting fire through his blood and pumping his release into the rubber.

He wished like hell he could shoot straight into Will's ass, fill him up with fresh semen. He didn't know why, exactly. It was probably some stupid *me Tarzan* thing.

Speaking of . . .

He pulled out of Will's body, stripped off the condom, and tossed it into the dirt. Before Will could notice and lecture him about littering—like he wasn't gonna pick it up later—he dropped to the ground and crawled between Will's widespread legs, then turned to face his hard, dripping cock.

"Come on my face," he ordered, staring up into Will's glazed eyes.

Will blinked. Once, twice, like he didn't quite understand. Then his teeth dug into his bottom lip, he took his prick in one hand and started jacking himself like the world would end if he didn't come in the next two minutes.

It didn't take two minutes. More like thirty seconds. Will's eyes rolled back, and he moaned sweet and low as his come splashed all over Koichi's lips, chin, eyelids, and forehead. He shut his eyes and opened his mouth to catch as much as he could of the salty-bitter fluid.

God, it was good. So, so good, to kneel in the cool dirt at Will's feet and feel his release like rain on his face. Warm, thick, musky-male-smelling rain.

Okay, so it wasn't a perfect analogy. His brain wasn't at its best right after sex.

A deep, satisfied sigh alerted him to the fact that Will was finished. He opened his eyes in time to catch Will in his arms as he dropped to his knees.

Pulling Koichi close with one arm and cupping his cheek in the other hand, Will kissed him, slow and deep, never mind the spooge all over his lips. Koichi melted into it, happy as a cat in a sunbeam. He loved these long, unhurried postsex kisses, where everything went from sexual to comfortable, and he felt like he could stay here forever, safe in the circle of Will's arms, with the unspoken promise of his body pressing hard and warm and sweat-damp against Koichi's.

When he let himself think about it, it scared him a little how quickly and completely he'd let down his guard with Will. How far he'd let this man he barely knew into his life. Will didn't believe he had. He could tell. But it was true. No one other than his twin had ever gotten behind his walls before.

If only he could figure out how to tell Will that.

Just say it, genius. No time like the present.

He wasn't surprised that his personal Jiminy Cricket sounded like his sister right now. He'd always been better at listening to her than to himself.

He broke the kiss and rested his forehead on Will's, raking his fingers through Will's dripping hair. "I want to tell you something."

Will pulled back so suddenly Koichi nearly fell over. His eyes were wide, black holes in the flickering light of the torches. "What is it? What's wrong?"

He sounded positively panicked. Frowning, Koichi touched his cheek. "Nothing's wrong. Settle down, okay?"

"Okay. Yeah." Will breathed deep, in and out, and smiled the fakest smile Koichi had ever seen. "Sorry. What did you want to say?"

He's scared, Koichi realized, watching Will with forced detachment. *He thinks I'm gonna ditch him like that jackass Anthony did.*

Jealousy stabbed Koichi in the gut. After what Anthony had done, Will had still come here looking for him. Still had feelings for him, maybe?

No. No, he was with Koichi now. And he was afraid Koichi would turn out to be another Asshole Anthony. It was up to him to prove he wasn't.

Gathering his courage, Koichi planted both hands on Will's shoulders and stared right into his eyes. "I just wanted to say I'm glad we're together now. You . . ." *Say it, idiot, just fucking say it.* "Look, I know you're afraid because of what happened with Anthony. And in the past, in some other relationships, I've tended to kind of hold back. But I've never been closer to anyone than I am to you. Other than

Kimmy, I mean. And that's different, obviously. I'm not going to be like Anthony. I won't do that to you. So, like, don't be scared, okay?"

There was so much more swirling inside him, trying to attach to the right words. Trying to become things expressed instead of things hidden in the cobwebby corners of his mind. But he was new at this whole talking-it-out business. He was trying, as hard as he could. Hopefully Will would see that.

Judging by the shine in Will's eyes, the way he smiled like Koichi had done something phenomenal rather than stumbling his way through a half-assed speech any normal person ought to be able to say without blinking, he must've done something right. That was good enough for now.

Will might've said something. He looked like he was going to. But the not-so-distant *put-put-put* of a boat engine stopped him. He lifted his head. A spotlight swept through the brush above their heads, originating probably twenty yards away.

Will dropped, pushing Koichi to the wet earth with him. "Somebody's out there."

Koichi didn't think the tense whisper was warranted, never mind shoving him into the mud like whoever was in the boat had any clue they weren't alone. "It's probably hunters again." He pushed at Will's chest. "Let me up. Mosquito bites are one thing, but I do *not* want to have to pull leeches off my personal area."

Will ignored him. Bad, bad, bad. "They're getting closer. We should put out the torches. Stay here."

With that, Will jumped up, crept over to the nearest bug-control torch—naked as his womb liberation day—and snuffed it with the attached douser. He was on his way to the next one before Koichi could recover from his shock and indignation sufficiently to peel himself out of the mud.

He pulled on his shorts and sandals before stumbling through the briars and bushes after Will, who'd evidently lost his mind, since he was crouching bare-assed in the undergrowth, staring at whoever the fuck was out there. "Will, what the—"

Will's hand over his mouth shut him up. "Be quiet," Will whispered in his ear. "Watch."

Shooting Will a look that promised revenge later on, Koichi hid in the bushes beside him and peered out at the group of people gathered a couple dozen yards away, on the far side of a narrow creek.

Five men and a woman stood in a rough circle, talking. He couldn't hear what they were saying, but the faces he could see were dead serious. As he watched, the woman glanced around, reached into the messenger bag slung over her shoulder, and pulled out a small package wrapped in brown paper. She handed it to one of the men—a thin, hawk-nosed person who looked like he never stopped scowling. He snatched it from her, turned away, and immediately strode toward the sleek canoe waiting not far away. One of the other men handed the woman a thick envelope. She opened it, took out a stack of money, and started counting.

Koichi's mouth dropped open. What the hell? What sort of shady deal was going down here? He glanced at Will, who was staring at the group like they'd personally betrayed him somehow. He didn't look at Koichi.

Frowning, Koichi turned his attention back to whatever the fuck was happening out there. The money guy was following the first man to their boat. They climbed in, and it moved away without a sound.

Someone else is rowing, Koichi thought, watching the vessel slip like a shadow through the bog. That fact sent chills up his back. Just how illegal was this, that they needed to sneak into the bog by canoe at night? Getting lost was highly likely without a spotlight. So what the hell had he and Will just witnessed?

Will nudged his shoulder, taking his attention away from that particular mystery. The others—the woman and the three remaining men—were climbing on board a flatboat with a spotlight mounted on top. The engine revved, and the boat pulled away, the spotlight sweeping over the water and weeds.

Koichi and Will sat there for a few minutes, hiding behind their tangle of briars. Finally, when the light and motor noise had moved away and the normal sounds of a summer night had taken over, Koichi rose and peered over the tops of the bushes. He couldn't see a damn thing except mud, undergrowth, and moonlight on the water.

"What the fuck was *that*?" He aimed a questioning stare at Will, who stood beside him, gazing out over the bog like he wanted to follow the flatboat and ask some pretty pointed questions of his own. A strange, sinking feeling settled over Koichi. "Will? Do you know something about what just happened?"

He shook his head, slowly, like he was thinking about it. "No."

That didn't sound very convincing. Koichi moved closer and took Will's hand in his. "Do you *guess* something, then?"

Will must've heard the suspicion in his voice, because he tensed, blinked, and faced Koichi with a wry smile. "No. I was just trying to figure out what they were doing. It's pretty intriguing, right?"

"Well, that's one word for it. 'Weird' and 'kind of terrifying' are some other words I can think of." Koichi wiped sweat from his upper lip. "That was obviously some kind of illegal deal. Like maybe a drug deal or something."

Will shook his head, his brow furrowed. "We don't know that."

"We don't *know* anything. But nobody comes out here at night to meet up and exchange some mysterious package for a shitload of money." A thought occurred to him that raised the hairs on the back of his neck. "I hope they didn't see us."

"I'm sure they didn't. They didn't say anything." Will fell silent, gazing out into the swamp and obviously thinking hard.

Koichi studied him with a sense of apprehension. Did Will actually know something about this? Because he was acting very strange. "We need to call the police and report this as soon as we get back in cell phone range. In fact, maybe I ought to call it in right now." He started to turn, intending to call on the boat's radio.

Will stopped him with a hand on his arm. "I don't think that's necessary."

Koichi stared at him. "But we saw—"

"What? We saw what, exactly?"

"Oh, come on. Those people exchanged something for a shitload of money." Koichi gestured toward the spot where the two groups had met not five minutes ago.

"We have no idea what they were doing."

"Seriously? You saw the same thing I did. You know as well as I do that something fishy was going on."

"We can't call the police all the way out here because we saw a bunch of strangers trade some money for something we couldn't see, and we *think* it might've been illegal."

Something was off here. Something Koichi couldn't pin down. "Will—"

Before he could get any further than that, Will leaned in and pressed a swift kiss to his lips. "Let's go on back to camp. I brought brownies for dessert."

He pivoted and tromped through the undergrowth toward their tent. Koichi trailed in his wake, deep in thought. What the hell had just happened?

Unfortunately, Will's weird mood didn't go away that night, or the next day. Or the day after that. In fact, almost a week later, he was still jumpy as hell, short-tempered, and prone to long, brooding silences.

"I'm really starting to worry," Koichi told Kimmy as they were getting ready to open the Thursday after the bog trip. He broke open a roll of quarters into the cash register drawer. "This isn't like him. And I'm trying not to let it get on my nerves, but it's pretty irritating when he snaps at me for no reason."

"I can imagine." Kimmy, kneeling on the floor, spritzed the front of the glass display case with cleaner and wiped it down. "Joanie says he's doing the same thing in the shop. She's making him stay in the office so he won't piss off the customers."

Jesus. That made him worry even more. Not to mention the whole not-calling-the-cops business, which had been an ongoing source of tension between them ever since they'd returned from Hunter's Bog.

He opened a roll of dimes into the tray next to the quarters. "Well. Obviously me being Mr. Nice Guy isn't helping. I'm gonna have to bite the bullet and make him tell me what in the seven hells is wrong."

Kimmy stood up and plunked her bottle of glass cleaner on the counter. "So you've tried talking to him?"

"Yeah, for all the good it does. I say, 'What's wrong?' He says, 'Nothin.' I say, 'You okay?' He says, 'Fine.'" Shaking his head, Koichi shut the cash drawer. "I didn't want to push him if he didn't want to talk. But, damn it, this is getting out of hand. I'll just have to force the issue."

"I know you don't want to, but I think you're right." She took his hand and squeezed. "Sorry, T."

"Thanks." Filled with a sudden flood of brotherly affection, he leaned over the counter and kissed her forehead. "And thank you, by the way, for always having my back."

She smiled, something softer and sweeter than her usual sharp, mischievous Kimmy-grin. "Hey, that's what twins are for, right? You've always got mine too."

"Better believe it. No one messes with my womb-mate but me."

She laughed. "That's why I love you—the terrible puns."

"I knew there had to be a reason." He let go of her hand. "I'm gonna run to the bathroom before we open. Be right back."

"Okay."

He was exiting the tiny one-seater bathroom in the back a couple of minutes later when he spotted Will standing in the rear parking lot, staring out at the bog. His posture was tense and stiff.

Dread settled in the pit of Koichi's stomach. Will had been quiet and gloomy this morning, like he'd been all week. But they hadn't fought or anything. In fact, they'd barely spoken. Koichi had been a little afraid to interrupt whatever dark thoughts were going on behind Will's thundercloud expression.

So what had happened between their arrival at the shops half an hour ago and now?

Well, you just said you had to talk to him. Looks like now might be the time.

Shit.

"What're you looking at?"

Koichi nearly jumped out of his skin. He turned to face Kimmy, one hand pressed to his chest. "Christ almighty, you scared the crap out of me."

"You should pay more attention. I wasn't exactly sneaking up on you." She leaned sideways to look out the screen door. "Is that Will?"

He nodded. "I think I'm gonna go talk to him."

Kimmy understood, thank God. She grabbed him into a tight hug. "Good luck. I love you, and I love Will. Make it better, okay?"

"I'll do my best." He pressed his cheek to her hair for a second, breathing the familiar scent of her citrus shampoo. "Love you too."

She let him go, her *go get 'em* smile on her face. He squared his shoulders and walked out the door into the parking lot.

Will half turned when the door slammed. "Hi, Koichi."

He speaks!

Koichi kept that to himself, since sarcasm was unlikely to help. "Hi." He went to stand beside Will. It was nice out, the morning warm but not yet unbearably hot. The breeze stirred through the reeds with a papery whisper, bringing with it the wet smell of the marsh. It felt cool, like rain in the future. "Why're you out here?"

Will's lips twisted into a bitter half smile. He peered at the ground like it had done something interesting. "Joanie kicked me out. Said I was being too absentminded to work in the shop today."

"Oh." More worried than ever, Koichi touched Will's hand. "Are you all right?"

Will shrugged. Didn't speak. Didn't even look up.

Okay then. No point in beating around the bush.

Steeling himself for a confrontation, Koichi faced Will, staring holes in his profile. "Something's been bothering you ever since our camping trip last week. Something besides the whole business about not calling the police. Every time I've asked, you've told me you're fine, nothing's wrong. I know that's not true, and I'm worried about you. So I want you to come clean with me. Right now. Tell me what's going on."

Will's shoulders drooped. He sucked on his lower lip. Let it go.

Koichi stepped closer and slipped his arm around Will's waist. "Look, I can tell this is hard for you. But whatever it is, you can trust me with it. I want to help."

Will opened his eyes. He didn't look at Koichi, but his face was set in determined lines. "It's about those people we saw in the swamp last week."

"Okay." Koichi's stomach knotted. *I knew it. Will knows something about what happened. Christ, he's not involved, is he?*

Drawing a deep breath, Will lifted his head and met Koichi's gaze. "One of them was Anthony."

CHAPTER 11

Will watched as shock, disbelief, and hurt chased each other across Koichi's face. Not that he'd expected anything different. Still, he'd dreaded this moment. Had done his best, in fact, to avoid it.

He should've known Koichi wouldn't allow that.

"Are you sure it was him? I mean, it was dark, and we were kind of far away." Koichi said it gently, without accusation or judgment, which was more than Will had expected. More than he deserved, honestly.

Still, he knew what he'd seen. "I'm sure. It was him."

Koichi's jaw tightened. His fingers curled against the small of Will's back. "It's been two years. People change."

That was true. But he'd spent a year and a half of his life loving Anthony. He knew Anthony's face as intimately as he knew his own. Feeling annoyed and defensive and ashamed of himself for it, he stepped away from Koichi's touch. "It was him. I'm positive."

Koichi sighed and rubbed his hands over his face. "Okay, so you're sure. But Will..." He chewed on his thumbnail, watching Will with understandable anger and less understandable sympathy in his eyes, and Will knew what he going to say before he said it. "What was he doing out there with those people, exchanging a mysterious package for money?"

"Anthony would never do anything illegal." Will kept his voice even with an effort.

Koichi pursed his lips. "You never know what people might do, or why."

"I was with him for a year and a half. I know him. You don't. And I *know* what he would and wouldn't do."

As soon as he said it, Will knew he'd let his rising temper get the better of him. But it was too late.

Koichi's cheeks flushed and his eyes glittered. "Well, I guess now I know why you didn't want to call the cops that night."

That cut, mostly because Koichi was right. Will crossed his arms and stared at the pulse throbbing in Koichi's throat. "We didn't see anything. Not really. And believe me, I know how I sound right now, but I swear to you, Anthony would never do anything illegal."

"I'd think you of all people would realize you don't always know people as well as you think you do. They do all kinds of shit you didn't see coming."

Just like I didn't see what you were going to do to me, said the venom in Koichi's voice. Will rubbed at the ache in his heart. "That was low."

"Yeah, well." Koichi looked away, his face tight and shut down. "I feel like you're hanging on to something that doesn't exist anymore. Like you're . . ." He swept one hand through the air in a frustrated gesture. "Like you're chasing a ghost. Like I'm nothing but a substitute for what you really want."

Will stared. "That's ridiculous."

"Is it?" Koichi pinned him with a narrow-eyed look. "If Anthony walked up right now and said he wanted you back, what would you do?"

Will wanted to insist that while he'd be happy Anthony was alive and well—though he already knew that much—he wouldn't go back to him. That it was far too late for a reconciliation. But the words wouldn't come out, and he wasn't sure why. Confused and a little scared, he dropped his gaze to the asphalt at his feet.

Koichi barked out a bitter laugh. "That's what I thought." He stalked toward his shop's door, then turned and strode back. "Decide what you want, Will. When you're ready to let go of the guy who *fucking left you* two years ago, you know where I live. Otherwise, I'm sure you can afford your own place by now." He spun and marched away. This time, he didn't stop.

The echoing slam of the shop door felt horribly final. Will wrapped his arms around himself, trying to kill the ache inside.

Eventually, he sneaked into his office for his truck keys and drove back to the gazebo in the park. This time, the weather was bright and sunny, though the fitful breeze smelled like threatening rain. People strolled through the grass with their dogs, and kids ran back and forth shouting to each other, playing whatever imaginary games children played.

Will envied them. He'd never had that kind of easy happiness. Not as a child, separated from his much older siblings and too awkward and shy to talk to the few other kids his age his parents ever allowed him around. Not even in college, where he'd finally come out of his shell enough to make friends and have his first relationship, but only with enormous effort on his part.

He'd come so close with Koichi. Then he had to screw it all up.

God, he was an idiot.

For nearly two hours, he sat there watching the kids and the dogs and the people walking around, and tried to work out what to do. He wanted to be with Koichi. But seeing Anthony in the bog last week—truly seeing him, solid and real, for the first time in two years—had thrown everything off-kilter. It had brought back feelings he'd thought he'd finally left behind. How could he be sure of his relationship with Koichi when simply laying eyes on Anthony could put his emotions in such a tailspin?

Where *was* Anthony, anyway? Obviously he was living around here someplace. So why hadn't Will seen him anywhere other than the bog?

Christ, was he actually living in the swamp? It was a horrific thought. But Anthony was an accomplished survivalist. If anyone could manage it, he could.

Something firm and wet hit his arm and bounced off. Startled, he looked around. A German shepherd bounded up the gazebo steps, snatched a ragged tennis ball off the boards at Will's feet with its mouth, and raced back into the park, where a little girl with a head full of tiny braids waited, jumping up and down and laughing.

Will watched the child and her dog with a wistfulness he hadn't felt in a long time. Normally, he wasn't the type to look back. The past was the past. No point in dwelling on it. But right now, he'd give a kidney to turn back the clock to his childhood. It hadn't been perfect.

He'd been a lonely kid. He'd known he was different from most other boys, though he hadn't known why until much later. But at least he'd been able to lose himself in the simple joy of playing fetch with his dog.

He wished like hell that forgetting his problems was still that easy.

Although apparently bumming around the park successfully distracted him from making important decisions. Like whether to keep living with his boyfriend, or allow them both their space while he got his shit together.

He knew what his heart wanted. He also knew what was best. Unfortunately, they weren't the same thing.

And you'll never get it done by sitting here brooding. Just rip off the damn Band-Aid already.

He didn't want to. He was so tired. All he wanted to do was rest. Just lie down and sleep forever. But if he wanted to collect his things before Koichi got home—and he definitely did; running into Koichi at the house would be beyond uncomfortable—he needed to get a move-on.

With an effort, he pushed off the seat and dragged himself back to his truck.

When Koichi got home that night, he found a note propped on the kitchen table.

He didn't read it.

At least, not right away. First he went upstairs, stripped, and took a shower, leaving the bathroom door open so he could hear the music from his phone, hooked up to the portable speakers in the bedroom. He tried hard not to notice that his was the only shampoo bottle on the ledge of the old tub now, or that the cedar-scented soap Will used was gone. If he didn't look, he could avoid facing the inevitable for a few minutes longer.

After a shower lasting way longer than was necessary, he cleaned the tub, washed the dirty dishes piled in the kitchen sink, and shelved all the books he'd bought that had been stacking up in the den over the last few months.

Eventually, though, he ran out of distractions. With nothing left to occupy his hands and his mind, and no desire to go to sleep yet, he finally steeled himself for whatever Will had decided to say when he'd crept in to clear himself out of Koichi's life.

Naturally, Will had known where to find the extra house key.

Betrayal stabbed Koichi in the gut. That probably wasn't fair, but there it was anyway. The first time he ever showed anyone outside his family where he kept his key, and he'd ended up putting his trust in the wrong man.

Thinking of the house key gave him another project, which he embarked on with enormous gratitude. He switched on the backyard light and went outside. The night was hot, still, and sticky. Crickets buzzed in the bushes. The neighbor's cat, Miss Havisham, ran across the edge of his porch, giving him her usual *come near me and I bite you* glare on the way. He waited until she'd vanished into the black shadows at the back of his yard, then fetched his extra key from underneath the zombie garden gnome that had guarded it for years.

He turned in a circle, wondering where to put it now. Someplace Will wouldn't think to look.

If he came back. Which he probably wouldn't.

Koichi couldn't decide which was sadder—him standing in his backyard at eleven fifteen at night hiding his key from Will, or knowing Will likely wouldn't ever come looking for it.

A roach as long as his thumb skittered across his bare foot. He squealed and jumped backward, shuddering all over. Fuck it. He dropped the key into the hanging fern and ran for the bug-free indoors. He could find a better hiding place tomorrow.

The reason he'd been stalling all this time came back to him when he got into his breakfast nook and saw the piece of paper with his name scrawled on it in Will's big, loopy handwriting propped against the salt shaker. *Read me*, it whispered. *You can't avoid me forever. Man up and do it.*

Crap.

He snatched up the note and sat down to read.

I thought about waiting until you got home, Will's message said without preamble, *but I figured it would be easier for both of us this way.*

I need some time to think and get my shit together, and it's probably best if we're not on top of each other while I do that. Sorry I'm such a fuck up.

Don't give up on us, Koichi. I haven't.

That was all. The note ended without any sort of signing-off. Hurt and fury formed a hard knot in Koichi's chest as he read the last two lines again. Don't give up? This coming from the guy who'd seen his old lover *one time*—okay, twice, maybe—from a distance and immediately started questioning his current relationship.

Koichi wadded up the note and threw it at the wall. It bounced off with a barely audible *tick*. Which was annoying, though hardly unexpected. He really felt like breaking something right now. Throwing paper was a piss-poor substitute.

His phone made a *zing-thonk* arrow sound, followed by Eric Idle announcing, "Message for you, sir!" He smiled. No one would text him this late except Kimmy.

He picked up his phone, thumbed it on, and brought up the new message. Sure enough, there was a goofy picture of her with eyes crossed and lips pushed out in an exaggerated duck face, next to a typically short text. *Hey. Haven't heard from U. Well?*

Sadly, he knew what she was asking. *He's gone.*

Shit. U ok?

No. But Ill live. If it was anyone else, he would've lied and said yes, he was fine. But he and Kimmy didn't do fake with each other. She'd understand, and she'd be there for him.

She messaged him again before he could even put his phone down. *Sorry hon. Call me if U want 2 talk.* ♥

K. Thanks sis.

No prob. C U 2morrow. Bye.

Bye.

He watched his phone's screen wink off, then sat there at his table for a while longer, staring at nothing and listening to the old fridge hum. Funny, how fast you got used to having another person around. Someone to talk to. Laugh with. Drive away the silence and loneliness.

Funny how another person could get so deep under your skin that before you knew it, you'd fallen in love with him, even though he was too stuck in the past to feel the same.

"Idiot," he told himself. "Stupid, fucking idiot."

Throat tight and aching, he shoved his chair backward, stood, and dragged himself upstairs. All he wanted was to sleep, and forget.

Naturally, it wasn't that easy.

Three days later, he'd worked out a complicated daily routine that included simultaneously avoiding Will and watching him on the down-low as often as possible. The upshot being that, between the planning, the avoiding, and the spying, he thought about Will pretty much nonstop.

Throw in the heartache that had settled inside him—boots off, feet on the table, all set to stay awhile—and what was left was a barely functional mess walking around in his skin.

God, he hated that.

Kimmy did too, he knew, though she was nice enough not to give him much grief over his gloominess. "You *could* go over there and talk to him instead of moping around all the time," she suggested during inventory Sunday morning. She shot him a meaningful look through an empty spot on the storeroom shelf. "He's not exactly Mr. Sunshine either lately. I think it's pretty obvious y'all need to work things out."

"And I already told you, his note said he wanted to work things out for himself. Without me." Would that ever stop feeling like a gut punch? "Five boxes of sage left. Those're selling fast. You might want to reorder."

"Order sage. Got it." She made a note on her iPad, half her attention still on him. "Don't you think he at least deserves to know you're in love with him?"

Koichi's heart lurched. He stared at the half-empty shelf below the one where they kept the sage. Business was going well, but that meant they needed to restock. Soon.

"Koichi? Honey, c'mon. Talk to me."

He rubbed his itchy eyes. Damn the dust back here anyway. "Who says I love him?"

This time, her voice was a tad sharper. "Don't pull that shit with me. I *know* you. Hell, I probably figured it out before you did."

She probably had. Which was just pathetic.

Planting his elbows on the shelf, he rested his chin in his hands and peered mournfully at his sister. "What am I gonna do, Kimmy?"

Sympathy flowed over her face. "Talk to him. Tell him how you feel."

The idea filled him with a toxic brew of longing and terror. "Even if he wanted to see me, which he doesn't, I'm not going to beg for anybody's attention."

She rolled her eyes. "Who said you should? Just tell him you love him, that the ball's in his court, and leave it at that."

It could work. He scratched behind his ear, turning the thought over in his mind.

Kimmy kept talking. "And from what you told me about the note he left, he didn't say he didn't want to *see* you, he said he thought it would be better if y'all weren't *living* together."

Damn her and her perfect memory. "I'm reading between the lines."

"No, you're overreacting." She smacked him on the arm. "Stop being childish. Go talk to him."

Staring at his twin across the storeroom shelf, he suddenly knew why he'd been avoiding it. The real reason, not the ones he'd been telling himself, and telling Kimmy. "I'm scared."

The look in her eyes said she didn't need to ask, but she did anyway. "Why?"

His eyes stung. He blinked until they stopped. "What if he doesn't love me back?"

Setting her iPad on the shelf, she framed his face in her palms, leaned over on tiptoe, and kissed his forehead. He rested his hands over hers. She didn't try to reassure him that *of course* Will loved him, thank God. He didn't want pretty lies.

Her silent support gave him the courage he needed, which was probably the point. "You're right. He ought to know. I'll talk to him." A fresh wave of fear rolled through his blood. "But I'm really fucking terrified."

"I know." She stroked his hair, her gaze holding his. "You're strong, Chichi. You can do this."

He wished he had her certainty. Yeah, he could face Will and make himself say those three life-changing words. But he wasn't so sure he could handle having Will confirm what he already suspected—that Will didn't return his feelings. How could he, if he needed to be apart to think things out?

Stop being a coward. You told yourself you'd try to open up more. That means not doing it only when it's easy.

Nodding to himself, he pulled Kimmy's hands off his cheeks and kissed her knuckles. "Okay. No point in putting it off. I'm going over there right now. Wish me luck."

"Of course." She ran around the end of the shelf, threw her arms around his neck, and hugged him hard. "I'm with you in spirit, hon. Good luck."

"Thanks." He plastered on his bravest smile, let her go, and marched out the back door like he was heading for his own execution.

Joanie answered his knock on the rear door of Will's shop. "Come on in, Koichi." She touched his arm as he walked in, her brow creased in concern. "It's great to see you. Are you okay?"

"Yeah, I'm fine." She was a sweet woman, and he liked her a lot, but he didn't know her nearly well enough to discuss his man troubles with her. Especially when those troubles involved her boss. "Is Will here?"

"He's out front, getting things in order." She wrinkled her nose. "He's been a real bear lately. It makes me nervous for him to interact with customers, but there's no stopping him, really. It *is* his shop, after all."

Koichi laughed, the sound soft and bitter. "I hear you. He's a stubborn one."

She studied him for a long, solemn moment, but didn't comment. "I'll let him know you're here. Hang on." She turned and glided down the short hallway toward the front of the store.

Koichi waited. A few seconds later Joanie returned, a smile on her face. "Go on in. I think he'll be very happy to see you."

He wasn't so sure, but his pulse thumped faster anyway. "Thanks, Joanie."

She nodded, then headed for the office. Koichi wiped his damp palms on his jeans. *Do it, you idiot. Don't stand here like a jackass.*

Drawing a deep breath, he squared his shoulders and strode into the shop.

Will waited for him beside the tent display, heartbreakingly handsome in a pair of black cargo pants and a snug blue Hood's Luxury Outdoor Expeditions & Supplies T-shirt that showed off his muscles. His mouth curved into a sad little half smile. "Hey, Koichi. How are you?"

For a single, blinding second, Koichi had to fight the urge to run forward, screaming like a berserker, and punch him in the mouth. *How are you?* Like they were strangers. Like they'd never had frantic, blistering shower sex, or cuddled together in bed on rainy nights, or told each other stories about the stupid things they'd done when they were kids.

But he hadn't come here to fight. And no doubt Will was saying the wrong thing because he felt as awkward as Koichi did. That being the case, the right thing to do was let it go and say what he'd come here to say.

"I'm . . . fine. I'm fine." Nervous, he picked at the loose thread hanging from his jeans pocket. "Look, I need to tell you something, and I need to do it before I lose my nerve. So just listen, okay?"

"Okay." Will took a step forward and stopped, watching Koichi with wide brown eyes. "What is it?"

Koichi's heart galloped so fast it made him sick. He swallowed, stared at the floor, and spit it out. "I'm in love with you, Will. *Don't* say anything. Just don't. Let me finish first. I'll give you the time you need to work out whatever you need to work out, and decide how you feel. That's only fair. But I won't beg you to love me back, and I won't wait around while you try it on again with Anthony. If you decide you have to go back to him, then it's over between us."

Silence. He mustered the courage to look Will in the eye. Will's expression was thoughtful and serious. Giving Koichi's ultimatum due consideration, no doubt.

A cold, black despair sank in Koichi's soul. His instincts had been right. Will didn't love him.

Well. Better to face up to it now than to keep twisting in the wind. Right?

"I'm not sure how I feel right now," Will said, his voice soft and measured. "I know that's not what you want to hear, and I'm so, so sorry." His brows pulled together, the skin around his eyes crinkling as if he was in pain. "You're the last person in the world I'd ever want to hurt. You sure as hell don't deserve it. But I know you don't want me to lie to you either. So all I can say is, I need more time. Maybe that makes me a horrible person, but it's the truth."

He couldn't argue with that, no matter how deep it cut. He nodded. "Thanks for that."

Will took one more step forward. "Koichi—"

He stumbled backward. If Will touched him now, he'd fall apart. "No. We'll talk when you're ready, okay? Bye." Holding himself together with pure willpower, he turned his back on Will's worried, anguished face and walked out the back door as fast as he could without running.

He managed to get outside before the tears came. He sank down into the narrow strip of weeds beside the building's wall, buried his face in his hands, and cried.

CHAPTER 12

The rest of Will's day felt like fighting his way through quicksand filled with razor blades—slow and painful. He knew the conversation couldn't have gone any other way. Lying to Koichi wasn't an option, and he wasn't yet sure enough of his feelings to say anything. But, God, it had hurt to see the pain in Koichi's eyes. He'd tried to hide it, of course, but Will knew his face well enough by now to see the emotional wounds.

He hated that he'd been the one to inflict them.

He was in the office pretending to go over records or something—he wasn't up to dealing with customers just then—when Joanie knocked on the door. "Will? Can you come out here for a minute?"

His heart tried to climb out his mouth. "What is it?"

The half-open door swung wide. She walked in, hands clasped in front of her. "Not what you think. There's a woman out here who'd like to book a private trip."

Relief left him weak. "Okay. Well, good. Hook her up, then."

"Um." She glanced over her shoulder, then back at Will. "She wants to go tonight."

Will stared. Joanie shrugged.

He slouched in his chair with a heartfelt groan. They'd had people want to book private trips before, but never quite this last minute. "How many people?"

"She didn't say. She wanted to talk to you personally." Joanie shifted her weight from foot to foot. Her mouth twisted into a frown. "You want me to tell her no?"

Let me tell her no, said the taut, uncharacteristically nervous tone in her voice. Perversely, Joanie's reaction only made Will determined to get out there and take care of this himself.

"Naw, I'll come talk to her." He pushed back his chair and stood. "Don't worry, Joanie. I can handle it."

Her frown deepened. "I know. But you're not really going to let her book a trip for *tonight*, are you?"

"I'm not sure yet. I have to get the details first." He walked up to her, studying her fiercely furrowed brow. "What're you so worried about?"

"I don't know. Nothing, I guess." She sighed. "It's such a strange request. I don't like it."

He smiled. They hadn't known each other long, but he'd already learned that Joanie was suspicious of anything that fell outside the realm of the usual routine. "Yeah, it is, but that's okay. I'll deal with it." He sidestepped around her, since she didn't seem likely to move out of the doorway. "I bet she's willing to pay a lot of money for something this last minute."

"I guess."

He started down the hall to the shop floor. Joanie followed.

Clients wanting private glamps usually had *rich* written all over them, with their expensive polo shirts, designer shorts, and tennis-club tans. They inevitably reminded Will of his family. The woman waiting for him beside the checkout counter couldn't have been further from that if she'd tried. She wore a tan skirt, a navy-blue blouse, and sensible sandals. Her dark-blonde hair was pulled into a low ponytail. She could've been anywhere from thirty to fifty. He would've passed her on the street without even seeing her. She was so nondescript as to be nearly invisible.

His heart sank a little. It hadn't taken him long to get his hopes up for making some serious extra money on this thing, and this lady didn't have that *money* look.

Still, he could use a distraction. Maybe a spur-of-the-moment expedition would do the trick. And hell, he could be wrong about her finances. His dad had always told him he was too quick to judge by appearances. It was about the only thing he'd ever agreed with his father on.

Plastering on his friendly-shopkeeper smile, he sauntered forward with his hand out. "Hi there. I'm Will Hood, the owner. It's great to meet you, Ms. . . . ."

"Cindy Johnson. Thank you for agreeing to speak with me." She stepped toward him and grasped his hand.

He mentally took her measure while they shook. Her grip was firm, her smile was warm, and her blue eyes gazed directly into his with a frankness he liked immediately. "So, Ms. Johnson. Joanie tells me you'd like to take a group out on a glamp tonight?"

"That's right. I know it's an inconvenience, so I'm prepared to pay you twice your usual rate."

He nearly swallowed his tongue. "Uh. What?"

"I said, I can pay you twice your normal rate. For your trouble, you know." She tapped a finger against her chin. "I could pay you more, if that's what it takes. You see, I have friends in town that I haven't seen in a very long time, and I promised them I'd take them out into Hunter's Bog to see the ghosts."

Well, there was a new wrinkle. He hadn't taken any groups into the bog yet, though he'd begun advertising for it. Will rubbed his temple, where the beginnings of a headache had started to throb. "You want to go out in the bog?" He wasn't about to comment on the likelihood—or not—of seeing any ghosts.

"Well. Yes." Her cheeks went pink. "I have a boat with a shallow draft and enough space for everyone—there's only four of us, including me—but I realized only today that I have no idea where the safe camping areas are in the bog. Then my friend Dustin saw your ad in the paper and suggested I try asking you to take us."

"Ah. Okay."

"So, will you do it?" She clasped her hands together and widened her eyes at him. "Please?"

He laughed. "How can I say no to that face?"

She squealed and clapped her hands, which made him laugh harder. He wasn't going to tell her that the real reason he'd agreed wasn't her puppy-dog face, but his own need to get away. To keep himself busy. Out there in the bog, setting up tents and cooking and taking care of his clients, he wouldn't have time to think about the hurt and betrayal in Koichi's eyes, or what in the seven hells he was going to do to fix the whole ugly mess.

"So, what do we do?" She bounced on her toes, practically vibrating with excitement. "Where should we meet? Here? I have a boat!"

"Yes, you said." Will did his level best not to laugh at her enthusiasm, but it was hard. He didn't think he'd ever seen anyone so eager to go camping in a swamp. "Actually, do you know where Lain Park is?"

She nodded. "Is that where we'll be putting the boat in?"

"Yeah. Why don't we meet up there at around five thirty? Does that work for y'all?"

"That should be fine, yes. What should we bring?"

"Yourselves." He thought for a second. "And bug spray. I have torches that're supposed to keep the mosquitoes away, and they do all right, but bug spray is still a good idea. Also, if you have any particular food or drinks you want, feel free to bring them. Otherwise, I'll be cooking my special fried catfish and hush puppies made with local IPA."

She grinned ear to ear. "That sounds absolutely perfect. Thank you so, so much for doing this, Mr. Hood."

"Please, just Will."

"All right, Will. Call me Cindy." She looked away, digging through her purse. "How much do I owe you?"

He did the math in his head: four people for one night, doubled since she'd said she would pay that, then decided he'd deduct at least part of it since she had her own boat. Damn, he was going to have to invest in a good boat. Even if Koichi took him back at some point, it wouldn't be fair to borrow *Starbuck* for bog glamps.

"Seven hundred ought to cover it." He watched her, nervous. She could still say "no deal" and walk out.

Instead, her face lit up like a spotlight. "Wow, that's such a great deal! Are you sure that's enough?"

Privately, he figured it was only a great deal for him. But he kept that thought in his brain. He nodded, cool as ice cream in July. "Yeah, that's fine. I'm not charging you for boat fuel when you're the one supplying the boat."

Her eyes went all soft and sparkly. "Oh, you're such a *nice* man! Thank you." To his surprise, she bounded toward him, rose on tiptoe, and kissed his cheek. She pressed a wad of folded bills into his hand.

He looked down. Seven one-hundred-dollar bills lay in his palm. For a second, he felt bad about how much he was charging. Then the businessman part of him grabbed the big-softie part of him by its nonexistent shoulders and gave it a good shake. If she couldn't afford this trip, she wouldn't have come here in the first place, and she sure as shit wouldn't have thought seven hundred bucks was a deal. Which, in all honesty, it sort of was, when he thought about it.

He smiled down at her. "Believe me, Cindy, it's my pleasure. I'll see you at the park at five thirty."

"Five thirty. Yes." She did another bounce-clap-and-squeal combo, grinning like a little girl on her birthday. "We'll see you then, Will. You have no idea how much this means to us. Thank you."

With that, she whirled around and floated out the door. Will shoved the money in his pocket and trotted toward his office, feeling a whole lot happier than he had fifteen minutes ago. Maybe it was stupid, but he liked having a project to occupy his mind and keep him from dwelling on things he couldn't change.

The money didn't hurt either.

"Joanie! I need you to man the front desk."

She came into view from the storage room, a box of the popular tin lanterns in her arms and an unhappy expression on her face. "You took the job, didn't you?"

"Yes, I did." He lifted the box, which was really too bulky for her to easily carry, and turned around to take it out front. "I'm meeting them at Lain Park at five thirty. We'll be camping at the spot in Hunter's Bog where Koichi and I usually go. She has a boat," he added, in answer to what he knew she must be thinking.

She sighed. "I wish you'd buy some radios."

"I will. In fact, I'll go get some tomorrow." He knew he needed to. Cell phones didn't work in the bog, so he needed communication in case of an emergency. Which was one reason he hadn't taken any official groups out in the bog yet. "I'll be sure to tell Cindy that we're cut off from communication, and have them all sign waivers."

"Well, it's something, I suppose." She laid a hand on his arm as soon as he set down the box, and aimed her troubled gaze at him.

"I know why you're doing this, Will. But I wish you wouldn't. I'm worried about you."

Part of him loved her for that. Another part wanted to hide from her well-meaning concern.

He grasped her hands in his. "I appreciate that. But I'm okay. I swear. It's good for me to get outside. That's how I deal with things." He dug into his back pocket, pulled out the bills, and held them in front of her face. "Seven hundred bucks up front, Joanie. Argue with *that*."

She narrowed her eyes at the money. Peered back at him. "The money's great. But I'm not worried about money." She touched his hand. "Just be careful, okay?"

Not for the first time, Will was glad he'd hired her. She was good for his business, sure, but she was also good for *him*. She reminded him that he wasn't alone. That people cared about him.

"I will. I promise, this is the best thing I can do for myself." He squeezed her hand. "Stop worrying, okay?"

She stared at him for a second, thoughtfully, like she was trying to figure him out. He held her gaze and tried to appear innocuous. Finally, she turned away, her shoulders slumped. "Fine. But if you get killed out there, I reserve the right to say I told you so."

He laughed, though it felt stilted and strange. "I'll give you that."

Silence fell. Will cleared his throat. "Well. Guess I'd better start getting everything together for tonight."

"All right." Joanie opened the box and pulled out a tin lantern. She didn't look at Will. "Let me know what time to expect you back tomorrow. Otherwise, I'm calling the police if you're not here by noon."

It was plenty of time. Will nodded. "I'll text you before we leave the park."

"All right. Thank you." She set the lantern on the display table. "I hope this helps."

"Me too."

She turned toward him. For a second they regarded each other in solemn silence. Then he turned and strode back to the office. He had preparations to make.

Cindy's friends turned out to be a lot like her: quietly friendly and effusively appreciative of everything he did. Dustin, Elaine, and Wallace—no last names given—plied him with questions about his business, his background, and once they learned he was a recent transplant, what he thought about the area. He answered them with as much patience as he could dredge up. They clearly didn't intend to pry, and he hated to be short with them.

Still, seeing the campsite come into view ahead was a relief. "Excuse me," he said, forcing his face into a smile. "But we're here. Cindy, you can pull up on that little beach there."

"Oh, perfect." She beamed over her shoulder at her friends. "Isn't it adorable, y'all?"

"Cute as a bug." Dustin grinned, putting a fine network of wrinkles in his cheeks and around his eyes. "Though I'm hoping there won't be too many *actual* bugs."

Will smiled at him. "Not as many as you might think. You won't get through the night without a few insect encounters, though."

Elaine—a tall black woman with a sharp, assessing intelligence behind her quick laugh and sweet smile—patted Dustin's shoulder. "Don't worry, Dustin. I'll protect you from the big, bad bugs."

The whole group laughed. Cindy nudged the boat up onto the sand. Wallace, the youngest of the bunch by several years, jumped into the shallow water. Will followed, and the two of them tugged the craft up the beach a few feet, making sure she wouldn't drift.

Will splashed back to the rear to climb back aboard and fetch his cookstove. He and Koichi had rigged a system of getting it off the boat and onto the land without breaking any backs or pulling any muscles, but it required one person on the boat and one in the water. He'd already explained the system to Wallace, who'd agreed to help.

The last thing he expected when he climbed up the rear ladder was Cindy pointing a gun in his face. Startled, he fell backward into the water, landed on his side, struggled to right himself, and came face-to-face with another weapon.

He froze. Wallace smiled at him. "Might as well settle down, Will. We're gonna be here for a while."

Will looked around. Elaine and Dustin jumped off the boat, both with weapons drawn and the golly-gee-aren't-we-swell acts dropped.

Wallace gestured with his gun. Will splashed out of the water onto the beach, four guns pointed at him and pure terror pumping through his blood.

What the hell was happening?

CHAPTER 13

Kimmy wanted Koichi to go home right away after the whole fiasco with Will, but he flat-out refused. Partly because he'd lose his shit at home alone with nothing to do but brood. But also because if Koichi wasn't there to stop her, Kimmy might actually go talk to Will in a misguided attempt to fix things between him and Koichi. Not that Koichi didn't appreciate the thought, but Will didn't deserve the invasion of his privacy—even if it would've worked, which was unlikely.

Besides, Koichi figured he was a little too old for his sister to be running interference in his relationships.

That decision made for a hell of a long day, though, even for a Sunday. By the time six o'clock rolled around, his cheeks ached from forcing himself to smile and the need to punch a wall itched inside him. Dropping the friendly-shop-owner act was a huge relief.

"You gonna be okay?" Kimmy asked as they walked out to their cars together. "You can come stay with me tonight if you want. Or I can stay with you. Maybe you ought not be alone."

"No, I'll be fine." He took her hand and squeezed. "Don't worry. I just need to curse his name in private for a while."

She didn't laugh, which told him he hadn't fooled her with his attempt at levity. "I get the cursing his name thing. I don't blame you one bit, especially since he's pretty much leaving you in limbo here. But I know you, hon. You want to hate him, but you can't. You're grieving, and you have to acknowledge that."

I do not, said the stubborn Koichi who didn't want to deal with any of it. But the more sensible Koichi knew she was right.

He sighed. "I know. And I love you for being there for me, sis, I really do. I just need to be by myself right now. Okay?"

"Yeah. Whatever you need, Chichi." She stopped, wrapped her arms around him, and hugged him tight. "I love you more than anything, brother of mine. Don't forget that."

His throat constricted and his vision blurred. "Never. The feeling's mutual." He gathered her into his arms and kissed her forehead. "See you tomorrow. And don't worry, I'll call if I need you."

"You'd better." She drew back, smiling. "See you."

They went to their separate vehicles. Kimmy waved as she drove away in her truck. Koichi watched her go, then started his car and headed home.

For the first time he could remember, his house looked cold and forbidding instead of inviting. That was a bad sign. The sun was still up. His house shouldn't look anything but welcoming in the daytime.

He sighed as he parked under the big oak tree at the end of the driveway. "This is gonna be a long night." Maybe Netflix had something he hadn't seen five times yet. With Will gone, he'd been catching up on his TV watching.

Funny how that didn't make him feel any better.

When he opened his back door, still pondering how to spend the long, empty hours ahead of him, he hardly had time to register the shape to his left in the dark room before it rushed at him and tackled him to the floor.

In the brief seconds of chaos and struggle that followed, he thought he glimpsed two separate people. Or at least, two sets of jean-and-boot-clad legs. Then someone pulled a piece of fabric over his head—red, he thought, closely woven—and tied something tight across his eyes so he couldn't see through it. Hands secured his wrists behind his back with what felt like plastic, and bound his ankles.

It all happened so fast, the idea that persons unknown had waited for him and attacked him *in his house* didn't hit him until his assailants lifted him by his elbows and set him in a chair.

Mouth dry and heart thumping in his throat, he summoned all his courage to speak as calmly as he could. "Who are you? What do you want?"

"You don't need to know who we are." Female, no accent, no inflection, flat and emotionless. The mental image of a cyborg popped into his head. "We want the missing pages."

The what? He shook his head, honestly puzzled. "I don't know what you mean."

Without warning, a fist slammed into his jaw, snapping his head sideways and rocking him in the chair. He sat there for a second, dazed, ears ringing. He forced himself to analyze the punch. Male, he thought. Not only because of the force of it, but the steep angle, and the size of the fist. Hell, maybe he was wrong, but the mental exercise kept his brain online, and he got the strong impression that he couldn't let himself check out.

"Have you remembered?" The woman again, her tone robotic.

He sorted through his mind for something to say that wouldn't get him hit again. Then it came to him: she was talking about the journal.

These are the people who broke into my house.

Cold fear crept along Koichi's nerve endings. They'd stolen from him, trashed his house, most likely burned down the old shop. What were they after, really? And what were they willing to do to get it?

"I don't know where the pages are," he said, truthfully. "I didn't know there *were* missing pages. I don't know any French, so I didn't ever know what it said."

He braced himself for another blow. It didn't come. Cyborg Woman spoke again. "We need the pages. You had the journal for many years. You must know or guess where they are."

"I honestly don't. Why would I lie? I thought the damn thing was worthless 'til you guys stole it."

If she found that argument convincing at all, she didn't say so. "We have Will Hood. If you don't tell us where the pages are, we'll kill him."

The threat hit Koichi like a kick in the gut. He bent forward, fighting nausea, his mind cycling between *thank God they didn't threaten my family* and *they can't hurt Will, they can't.*

"I swear I'm telling you the truth." His voice emerged in a shaking whisper. "I *swear.* I don't give a shit about the stupid journal or whatever you want with it. I'd give you those pages right now if I knew where they were, but I don't. Please, please just don't hurt Will, okay? Please."

Silence. Thick, dangerous silence. He swallowed bile.

"We will take you to Mr. Hood," said the woman.

He wasn't sure if that was better or not, but it was evidently the best he was going to get.

As a child, Will had often acted out perilous imaginary adventures on the grounds of his family's ranch. He'd played *captured by bad guys* more than once. But in those escapades, he'd never been afraid, and he'd always escaped.

Real life was horribly different.

The group he'd assumed to be customers had tied his hands behind his back and secured his bound wrists to his stove. Pretty clever, since it was way too heavy to drag along with him if he tried to run. They didn't bother to hide what they were talking about from him, and of course he'd already seen all of their faces. That made him nervous. It meant they didn't intend for him to get out of this alive.

Joanie knows where I am. She'll call the police if I'm not back tomorrow.

If tomorrow wasn't too late.

Cindy pulled up a camp chair and placed it in front of where he sat cross-legged in the grass. He watched her plant herself in the chair. "What the hell do you people want?"

She crossed one thin leg over the other and gave him a cool smile. "You and your friend Koichi McNab have been camping in this spot many times, is that correct?"

"Yeah." He studied her face, searching for answers. "Why do you want to know?"

She ignored his question. "Mr. McNab had an old journal. Some pages were missing. Do you know where they are?"

Huh? "No. I don't think he even knew there *were* pages missing. At least, he didn't tell me that. Maybe he didn't think it mattered."

"It did." She pursed her lips. "Hmm. I'll be frank with you, Will. We're searching for something that we believe to be in this area. If you and your friend have found anything unusual here, I need you to tell me, right now."

He held her gaze. "You'll kill me if I don't, right?"

THE SECRET OF HUNTER'S BOG

Dustin walked up to her and laid a hand on her shoulder. "They've got McNab. He says he doesn't know. They're getting ready to bring him here."

Her expression soured. "Well. It is what it is, I guess. Thank you."

"Sure." Dustin raised his eyebrows at Will, then turned and sauntered away.

Will glanced from Cindy to Dustin's retreating back, then to Cindy again. "What? What do you mean?"

"Exactly what it sounds like." She uncrossed her legs and leaned forward, elbows on her knees. "I'm sorry, Will. I really am. Nobody wanted it to happen like this. We wanted to be in and out, get that journal, find the jewels, and be gone. But sometimes things go wrong. And in this case, you and Koichi were in the wrong place at the wrong time."

Oh God. The camping trip in the bog when they'd seen the group making the exchange. When he'd seen Anthony.

They'd been spotted, and hadn't realized it.

Despair rose inside him like black water. "We didn't see anything, I swear. We saw lights, that's all. We didn't see any faces. Don't you think I would've recognized you? *All* of you?"

Her eyes softened with a sympathy he hated because he couldn't tell whether it was fake or real. "None of us were out there that night, Will. We know you wouldn't have taken us out here if you'd recognized us. But I know that you *did* see faces. Both of you did. No one wants this to happen, especially me. I don't want to kill you. I don't want that on my conscience. But it has to be done."

"We won't tell anyone. I promise. Neither of us will." He knew he was begging, but what choice did he have? If that's what it took to save his own life and Koichi's, he'd do it. "Why do you have to kill us?"

She peered at him with that calm, unyielding expression. "If you help us find what we're looking for, maybe you can live." She stood, brushing dirt off her shorts. "Think about it, Will. Think very, very hard. If you remember where those pages are, maybe we can spare your life, and his."

He watched her walk away, and knew this place was where he would die. He didn't have the information they wanted. Maybe he could make up a convincing lie, but it wouldn't matter. She'd only told him that to keep him from freaking out. If he stayed here, he would die.

And Koichi. Christ, they were going to kill Koichi too. That hurt worst of all. Because he'd wasted time waffling, chasing the past, wondering where his heart and his loyalties lay, when he knew the answer all along, if only he'd had the courage to look it in the eye.

He loved Koichi. Wanted to be with him. No one else, just him.

He wished it hadn't taken a threat to both their lives to make him see. But there it was.

The realization jolted him hard enough to clear the fog of fear from his mind and show him what he had to do. If only they'd leave him alone long enough to work on loosening his bonds, or at least to try to get the tether out from under the leg of the cookstove. He could bide his time until Koichi was here, then take them by surprise. Maybe get hold of one of the weapons if he could free his hands. He wasn't a great shot, but he wasn't bad either.

Slowly, carefully, watching his captors as unobtrusively as he could, Will began twisting his wrists.

Koichi's head cracked against the barely padded floor of the car's trunk for at least the twentieth time. He didn't bother to scream or curse this time. His throat burned from all the other times, and it wasn't like anyone would hear him. Cyborg Woman and her minions had lifted the bag over his head enough to stuff a scratchy, sour-tasting cloth in his mouth and tie it in place before carrying him outside and tossing him into the trunk of their car.

He hadn't seen any of it, of course, since they hadn't unblindfolded him. But he knew the sound of a car trunk opening and closing, and he knew it wasn't his. It sounded bigger. More substantial. Older. He wondered if they'd parked deep enough in the shadows to hide the kidnapping, or if any of his neighbors had seen and called the cops. They definitely wouldn't have heard his screams for help. He'd barely heard them himself.

With no way to measure time in his sensory deprivation, the drive seemed to last hours. Days. Eternities. Wherever they were taking him, the road there sucked. Or the car's shocks sucked. Or both. He'd already gathered an impressive collection of bumps and bruises to add to his swollen, aching jaw.

All the while, he worried about Will. What were they doing to him? What the hell did they *want*? Christ almighty, if he'd had any clue this sort of shit would happen, he'd have thrown away that stupid journal ages ago.

The car stopped suddenly, brakes squealing, the rear fishtailing. Koichi slid and slammed against the side of the trunk. Pain bloomed in his shoulder and spread down his arm.

He ignored it. Outside the car, voices shouted to "freeze" and "drop it" and "get on the ground."

Police.

Adrenaline shot through his blood, turning all his aches and pains into background noise. Squirming into a better position, he found metal with his feet and kicked as hard as he could, screaming at the top of his ruined voice. He had to get the cops' attention. *Had* to. Otherwise, who knew how long he'd stay locked up in here. Or what might happen to Will in the meantime.

Something went *pop* outside. More pops followed.

It took Koichi a minute to realize the sounds were gunshots.

Shit. Not good.

He stilled, heart racing. Should he keep kicking? Would that distract the police and get someone killed? He didn't know. Maybe he ought to wait until the firefight died down.

And what if Cyborg Woman and her boys killed the cops? What would they do to him then? Would it make it worse if he'd tried to get the attention of the police? Would it matter?

You're panicking. Stop it.

He tried to take deep breaths. Tried to force his body to relax, his pulse to slow. But it didn't work. How in the fuck was he supposed to stay calm when he was at the mercy of whoever won the battle? He'd never felt so helpless in his life.

When the trunk opened, he flinched and started worming his way to the rear of the trunk. He hated himself for it, but he couldn't help it. Every molecule in his body wanted to get away, and was by God going to try whether he liked it or not.

"Hey. It's okay," said an unfamiliar voice. "You're all right now. Let's get you out of there."

Careful hands helped him sit up, cut the bonds around his wrists and ankles, and removed the hood and gag. Koichi blinked and peered into a pair of sharp brown eyes in a round, bronze-skinned face.

Cop. No doubt. He had that indefinable air that screamed *law enforcement*.

"You okay?" The man gave him a once-over with that cop-look that saw everything. "Can you speak?"

"Yeah." The word was no more than a squeak. Koichi cleared his throat. "Who're you?" His voice emerged in a painful rasp. He grimaced.

"Special Agent Anthony Ruiz. FBI."

CHAPTER 14

Koichi stared, struck dumb. Anthony. *Will's* Anthony.

He wondered if Will knew the jerk who'd ditched him was FBI.

He wondered if that had anything to do with what had happened two years ago.

And why was Anthony here, anyway, apparently wound up in this whole thing with the house-robbing, shop-burning, journal-stealing kidnappers? Why was the FBI involved? What the ever-loving *fuck* was going on?

None of the thoughts pinging around Koichi's brainpan made it out of his mouth. They tangled into a confused knot and lodged hard in the back of his throat, leaving him gawping at Anthony Ruiz, FBI, like a damned idiot.

His questions must've shown on his face, because Anthony's mouth twisted into a wry smile. "We've been after these people for a while. The ones who kidnapped you are secondary players, but we're hoping they can take us to the ringleaders."

"Of what?" Talking hurt, but Koichi didn't give a shit. He wanted answers. "Why'd they grab me? Why'd they rob my house and my shop? And why'd they threaten to kill Will and me?"

Anthony's jaw tightened. "They threatened Will?"

"Yeah."

"Do they actually have him?"

Now that he thought about it, Koichi realized Cyborg Woman hadn't said. "I don't know. They said they'd take me to him, though. So I figured they did."

Anthony turned around and gestured to someone Koichi couldn't see. A woman with a bloodstain on her white blouse trotted over. Anthony murmured something to her. She nodded and jogged off again, with a quick look at Koichi.

He watched with a frown as she spoke to a uniformed cop who was taking pictures of a man lying on the ground in a lake of blood. "What's that about?"

"That's my partner. I asked her to send out units to find Will. We know of a few spots this bunch frequents in the bog. They might've taken him to one of them." Anthony sighed. "Who knows if it'll turn up anything. But we have to try something."

Koichi glanced around so he wouldn't have to see the fear and remorse in the other man's face. Now that he was paying attention, he saw that he sat in the trunk of an old black car parked beside an overgrown, poorly kept boat ramp. The setting sun glared orange on the still water. He didn't recognize the spot. "Where are we?"

"Private property being used by an antiquities collector." Anthony peered at Koichi with solemn eyes. "That person is who we're after. No one knows who exactly he or she is. The people who snatched you work for them."

The light dawned, and Koichi's jaw dropped open. "Oh shit. They're running illegal antiquities. Stealing 'em for this private collector."

Anthony nodded. "Whoever our target is, he or she is a dealer as well as a collector. The FBI was called in when antiquities were moved over state lines, and between countries."

"My grandmother's jewelry? I didn't think it was that old."

"From what I've gathered, it isn't. We've been watching this group for a long time because they've been dealing in Native American artifacts. The theft of your grandmother's jewelry and your perfume bottle were apparently a couple of their side projects." Anthony shrugged when Koichi gaped at him. "It's not the first time. They trade in other valuables once in a while. Those sorts of things are easier to sell."

Koichi rubbed his aching head. "When they tied me up, they questioned me about some missing pages from that stupid journal."

Anthony's gaze sharpened. "You know about the journal?"

"Yeah. They stole it from my house." He narrowed his eyes at Mr. FBI. "How do *you* know about it?"

Anthony looked away. "That's sort of a long story."

Realization hit Koichi like a brick to the head. "That's what you were exchanging in the bog that night. Will saw you."

Surprise and shame rolled over Anthony's face before he got his expression under control. "Yes. I've been working undercover, trying to get to the head of the ring. I haven't been able to catch them actually trading artifacts, and my team and I were hoping the journal trade might get me in on something more incriminating. I didn't realize anyone saw us that night. But I'm betting that's why you were grabbed. Or at least why Will was."

Renewed fear for Will's life clawed at Koichi's chest. "Can you find him before they hurt him?"

"I don't know. But I'm damn well going to try."

The steel in Anthony's voice matched the determination in his eyes, and Koichi began to see why Will was still stuck on him.

Koichi bowed his head because he couldn't stand to look at the man Will loved instead of him. "Can you let me know if you . . ." He stopped. Breathed. *Think positive.* "When he's safe? Please?"

"Of course." A siren wailed in the awkward silence that followed. Anthony glanced over his shoulder. "Ambulance is on the way. They'll look you over, then my partner will get your statement." He turned and strode toward a bullet-ridden car not far off.

Koichi watched him go. The flashing red lights of the two approaching ambulances made him look bold and dangerous. Jealousy curled in the pit of Koichi's stomach. It was stupid and petty, with Will's life on the line, but he couldn't help it. Why would Will choose him, when he was the one who'd caused the whole shit-storm in the first place—not on purpose, but still—while Anthony was the hero riding to the rescue?

As Anthony climbed into his car and drove off, tires squealing, Koichi saw Will in his mind's eye—Will's smile, his shining eyes, the way his mouth went soft and slack when he came. The thought of him being hurt—or killed—was unimaginable. He could live without Will, as long as Will was safe and happy.

Tears stung Koichi's eyes. He blinked them away as two paramedics walked toward him. *Please be okay, Will.*

By the time Cindy came back to the camp chair, Will had managed to work one of his hands free of the plastic tie. If he hadn't been tethered to the damned stove, he could've run even with the tie around his other wrist. But he was, so he couldn't.

He kept his poker face on while Cindy sat in the chair and crossed her legs. Blood trickled down his fingers from where he'd rubbed his wrists raw. The wounds burned like acid, but he ignored it. He couldn't let on what he'd done.

She smiled her cool smile that didn't touch her eyes. "Have you remembered anything useful, Will?"

He licked his lips, tasting sweat and trying to recall everything Koichi had told him about the journal. "I've been thinking, and I think that if the missing pages are the ones you really need, then it seems likely to me that Lamar took those pages with him when he vanished. Don't you think so?"

She nodded, her expression thoughtful. "Possible. Yes. He was the sort who would have done that."

"I could help you find the jewels."

Her eyebrows rose. He stared her down. He'd spoken on impulse, but if she took him up on it, he'd stay alive a little longer. Which would give him a greater chance to help Koichi too.

She shifted. Leaned forward. He thought she was about to speak. He held his breath.

The sound of a boat's motor cut through the quiet. Cindy rose. "That'll be our colleagues with Mr. McNab. Don't go anywhere." She smiled like that was funny, then hurried off toward the beach.

Will didn't wait. With Cindy and her cohorts all huddled around the landing spot and paying him no attention at all, this might be his last chance to escape. He turned, planted his free hand on the underside of the stove, and pushed. It fell into the sand with a clatter. He yanked the tether off the leg and ran into the trees without l ooking back.

He expected at least one of the group to hear. To follow him. Instead, a brilliant spotlight chased away the darkness before he'd gotten more than a few yards.

"FBI," boomed a megaphone-amplified voice. "Drop your weapons and get on the ground, facedown, hands behind your head. Do it now."

FBI? Will stopped and looked back. Behind the light, he could just make out the shape of a boat. As he watched, several people jumped into the water and splashed ashore, weapons aimed. He saw Cindy kneel in the sand, her hands up. An armed man shoved her facedown and started cuffing her. A few feet away, Elaine was getting the same treatment.

The hours of terror and tension drained out of him. He was safe now. All he had to do now was make sure the FBI knew that he'd been held captive, and that these people had Koichi held somewhere too.

Putting his hands in the air with palms open and out—he didn't want to get shot by mistake—he started walking slowly toward the beach. Wallace crashed through the underbrush and ran headlong into him. Startled, he grabbed the man and threw him to the ground more out of instinct than anything else. He barely managed to raise his hands again before an agent came racing after Wallace, her gun leading the way. She skidded to a stop when she spotted Will with his hands up and his foot on Wallace's back.

"They kidnapped me and threatened to kill me," Will said before she could speak. "I'm Will Hood. They have Koichi McNab too, and they threatened to kill him. You have to find him."

Another agent arrived as he finished talking. The two glanced at each other. The woman turned her attention back to him. "Back away, sir."

He did what she said. The two agents handcuffed Wallace, and the male agent dragged him off toward the boat, reading him his rights as they went.

The woman holstered her weapon. "I'm Agent Berry. Mr. McNab is safe." She hitched her head beach-ward. "C'mon. We have a medic with us. Let's get him to look at those wrists."

He followed, trembling with reaction now that it was all over. "How did you know to look for me here?"

"The agent in charge of this investigation gave us this location as one of four likely spots."

"So you checked all of them?"

"Yeah. Sent out teams to each spot." She cast him a grim look. "Good thing Agent Ruiz sent us here when he did."

Will stopped, stomach churning. "Agent Ruiz?"

"The agent in charge, yeah." Berry frowned at him. "You don't look so good. Here, sit down." She grabbed an overturned camp chair, planted it in the sand, and pushed Will into it.

He sat, since he didn't feel like his legs would hold him up much longer. "It's going to sound weird for me to ask this, but what's his first name?"

She eyed him like he'd asked her to tango, but didn't comment. "Anthony."

Oh God. That explained so much. Will leaned forward and buried his face in his hands.

Anthony was waiting in Lain Park when Agent Berry pulled the boat up to the public dock. He looked different than he had two years ago. Still handsome in his round-faced, youthful way. But his eyes held a hardness they hadn't before, and the new lines around his mouth spoke of a bitterness born from harsh experience.

He pushed away from the hood of the battered white pickup truck he'd been leaning on, cracking his knuckles the way he'd always done when he was nervous. Will stepped off the boat and walked down the dock toward his once-upon-a-time love, knees shaking and mouth dry. The truck looked familiar. Was it just because so many people here drove similarly well-used vehicles, or—

The answer hit him like a lightning bolt. He stopped in the weeds between the dock and the oyster-shell lot, staring at Anthony. "You saw me. In the park that day. You *saw* me. You *knew* it was me."

The *why didn't you talk to me* wouldn't come out, but Anthony had known him long enough and well enough to hear it anyway. "I was undercover, Will. I couldn't talk to you then. It would've screwed up everything." A half smile twisted Anthony's lips. "Seeing you there really threw me. All this time, I thought you were still in Houston."

"I was, up until a couple of months ago."

"What made you decide to move here?"

Agent Berry brushed past, killing the words on Will's tongue. He squinted up at the moths wheeling around the nearby streetlight.

"It's not a coincidence that we're both here," he said after she was out of earshot. "But I'm betting you already knew that."

Anthony nodded. "I figured, yeah."

Studying the familiar-yet-not face of the man he'd once loved, Will knew the time had arrived to get what he'd come here for. "I need to know once and for all what happened back then. I've blamed my father. I need to know if I'm right or wrong." Another agent strode by, hustling a handcuffed Cindy ahead of him. She cast Will a cold sidelong glance. He rubbed his arms, thinking of how close he'd come to dying tonight. "I haven't spoken to my father in a year and a half because I believed he drove you away. You owe me some answers."

"You're right. I do." Anthony stepped closer, peering at Will with eyes full of guilt and sorrow. "Look, you need to give a statement to Agent Berry, and I need to get some initial paperwork done. But after that, let's talk, okay? In private. I'll tell you everything." He touched Will's arm, a light brush of fingers that brought back painful memories of a thousand other touches, in another lifetime. "I'm truly sorry about what happened with your dad. I'd fix it, if I could."

Will managed a smile. "If it wasn't that, it would've been something else, eventually. He always thought I was weak because I had trouble reading, and talking to people. And I don't think it helped that I wasn't ever going to produce grandchildren."

The solemn expression didn't budge from Anthony's face. "Doesn't matter. Your falling out was my fault, and it didn't need to happen. I won't ever forget that."

Will didn't answer. He was starting to get an idea of what might've happened two years ago, and he didn't like it at all.

Anthony stepped back, stuffing his hands in his pockets. "Well. I'd offer you a ride to the police station, but something tells me you wouldn't take it right now. So I guess I'll catch up with you after we're both done with what we have to do."

With that, he spun on his heel and went back to the banged-up pickup. Will watched him until he'd driven out of the parking lot before going to his own truck.

Two and a half hours later, Will walked out of the Duchene police station into the warm, sticky night air, his nerves frayed to the breaking point. Now he got what the twins had been talking about before, when they'd been questioned about the fire and robbery at their old shop. He felt like his brain had been diced and examined under a microscope, and he was the *victim* here.

Well. One of them.

"Where's Koichi?" he asked when Anthony emerged behind him. "Did they question him too?"

"Yeah. He got done a while back. He ought to be home by now." Anthony fell into step beside him, walking with him to the small front parking lot. "If it makes you feel any better, he seemed very concerned about making sure you were safe. He wanted me to call him once we knew you were okay."

"Oh." Will stopped beside his truck, letting that process. It could mean everything, or nothing at all. Koichi wasn't the sort of person to wish him actual harm, no matter how angry or hurt he might be.

Sympathy shone in Anthony's eyes. "I had Agent Berry call him earlier and tell him we got you out safe. But I should probably call him myself and fill him in on the details. He'll worry."

"No, wait."

Anthony raised his eyebrows. Will stared him down. "He knows I'm okay. That's going to have to do for right now. You promised me answers, Anthony. Your place, or mine?"

Anthony rubbed at the stubble shadowing his jaw. "I'd love to see your shop."

Will frowned at him. "Wait, do . . . How do you . . ." He trailed off, his words deserting him.

A wry smile curved Anthony's lips. "FBI, remember? It didn't take much to figure out everything about you once I knew you were here."

Shit. Will sighed. "Fine. You can follow me." He unlocked his truck and climbed behind the wheel without another word. He wasn't sure how he felt about Anthony investigating him.

No, that wasn't true. He *was* sure. And he didn't like it.

He told Anthony so once they reached their destination, as they walked across the back parking lot of Hunter's Bog Mall.

"You're right," Anthony said. "I shouldn't have done that. But damn, it'd been *so long* since I'd seen you, and you just popped up here, where I'd been for the past nine months, and, well." He made a helpless gesture. "Can you honestly say you'd've done differently in my shoes?"

He couldn't. Especially since he'd done pretty much the same thing, following the random Instagram picture of Anthony here to Alabama.

He laughed, softly, sadly. "I guess I'd've done the same."

Anthony turned and strolled down the hallway to the front of the shop. "Nice tent," he called. "You're really sleeping here?"

"Yeah." Will seriously did not want to explain the whole sad story between him and Koichi. How he'd had something good, how he'd screwed it up by being stupid and indecisive, and how that had led him back to living in his shop again. "I just haven't gotten around to looking for something else yet."

Anthony was standing beside the tent when Will emerged from the hallway. His expression reminded Will of their last night together—grim, haunted, devastated. "I'm so sorry," he said before Will could get a word out. "We had something *precious* together. And I killed it. I'll regret that for as long as I live."

A hard ache lodged in Will's throat. He went to Anthony and took his hands. "For whatever it's worth, I forgave you a long time ago. But I get the feeling that you might be blaming yourself too much. Don't you think it's time you told me what happened?"

Anthony nodded. He gave Will's fingers a squeeze, let go, and turned to peer out the front window, arms wrapped around his own ribs like he was literally holding himself together. "I always wanted to be an FBI agent," he said, his voice soft and shaky. "Ever since I was a kid. After I graduated from college, I took the job on your dad's ranch because it paid well enough for me to afford my own place. Then I applied for special agent training as soon as the next application period opened. I didn't hear back, and I'd pretty much given up. Then two agents from the Houston field office came to my apartment and asked me if I'd be willing to work for them as an informant. The ranch foreman was under suspicion of drug trafficking, and they needed someone to gather information for them. And I was already working there. It was perfect, as far as they were concerned."

Will thought back to Barry Wells, who'd run the day-to-day operations of his father's business for twenty years. He'd never gotten along with the man, but he wouldn't have pegged him for a drug dealer. Another thought occurred to him, and he frowned. "They just got some kid off the street to do their dirty work for them?"

Anthony glanced over his shoulder. "I'd been earning a living working stables with my family since I was twelve, Will. I paid my way through college working in stables. I've managed more than one, you know. I wasn't a kid, and they didn't recruit me off the street."

"Okay, yeah. Sorry." Will raked a hand through his hair. "But, I mean, don't they have their own people to do this stuff? How'd they know they weren't putting you in danger?"

"They kept an eye on things. But one thing I've learned is that the FBI uses informants a lot." Anthony dropped his arms from around his waist. "Not usually to that extent. But they needed to be careful. They said the suspect had friends in high places. Resources. That he might be able to track down members of the Bureau. Which is why they wanted someone who was already working for the ranch. They said they thought I'd be accepted into special agent training, based on my application, and that made me the best choice as their informant." His voice dropped low. "They offered my parents citizenship in exchange for my help. I couldn't say no to that, even if I'd been inclined to turn them down in the first place."

A suspicion had formed in Will's mind while Anthony talked. "Was my dad involved? Was he the friend in high places?" Will dreaded the answer, but he had to ask.

"We're not sure. It's possible he was." Anthony turned to Will again. The anguish in his face hurt Will's heart. "The thing is, he found out not only that you and I were together, but that I was working with the FBI. I don't know how he got that information. My boss wouldn't tell me. He threatened to sue the agency and splash the whole thing all over the press unless they killed the investigation and sent me away. And sending me away had to be a part of the deal, apparently. I'd collected some information, but not nearly enough for them to prosecute. So they were forced to end the investigation."

He hung his head. "At least they kept their word and gave my parents their citizenship."

Will stared, fury and betrayal churning in his gut. "He knew? All this time, my father *knew* and didn't tell me?"

Anthony nodded. "It was my fault, though. There are reasons agents don't get involved with anyone connected to a job. I broke the rules."

"You weren't an agent then."

"No." One corner of Anthony's mouth tilted up. "There's a good reason why that's a rule, though. Look at how badly I hurt you. How I hurt *us*."

Will raked his hands through his hair. "How did my father even pull that off? How could he bully the FBI into giving up on an investigation? How does that even fucking *work*?" Rising anger and frustration sent him pacing, back and forth, back and forth, between the tent and the checkout desk. "I don't understand any of this."

Anthony laughed, a sound as sharp as broken glass. "They fucked up. They put a civilian informant in place in a key undercover position, and when it came right down to it, they couldn't defend that decision. Especially since they didn't have enough evidence to base a case on. So they had to back off."

Will wrinkled his nose. "I don't like it."

"Neither do I."

After all this time, after all his mixed emotions toward Anthony over the years, Will felt only sympathy for him now. He wished he'd known the true situation two years ago, if only so he could've kept Anthony from having to suffer the way he clearly had.

He no longer wished he could've saved their relationship. If he had, he wouldn't have met Koichi. And he wouldn't change that for anything.

Still, he wanted to take the sorrow and guilt out of Anthony's eyes. "You need to stop blaming yourself, Anthony. None of what happened was your fault."

Anthony hunched his shoulders. "None of it would've happened if I hadn't let myself get involved with you. We could've gotten the evidence and closed the case. Everything would've worked out the way it was supposed to."

"Maybe. Maybe not. You can't know that for sure." He grasped Anthony's hands again, holding on tight. "But listen. I'm glad for the time we had together. I'm a better person for it. I wouldn't change that. The only thing I would change, if I could, is how it all worked out for you, because you've obviously been carrying a lot of guilt around, and you shouldn't have to. Especially about my father." He shook his head. "I can't believe he did that. I don't know if I can forgive him or not."

"That's up to you. Although I think you might eventually regret it if you don't."

Will couldn't imagine that. "We'll see." He gave Anthony's hands a squeeze, then let go. "So what happened after Houston? I assume the FBI accepted your application, since you're an agent now."

"Yeah." Anthony smiled, his face lighting up. "I've been working with the antiquities task force ever since I graduated. It's tough work, but I love it."

His obvious happiness made Will smile too. "I'm really glad for you, Anthony. And it doesn't surprise me a bit. You always were awfully smart." A yawn hit out of nowhere, threatening to split his face in half. "Damn. Excuse me."

"You're tired. I should go." Anthony pulled him into a hard hug. "I'm so happy we got to talk."

"Me too." Will patted his back. They smiled at each other as they drew apart. "Listen, you said you were gonna call Koichi. I'll do it, okay?"

"Okay." Anthony arched an eyebrow. "I think he'll be very glad to hear from you."

I hope so. Will swallowed. "Thank you, Anthony. For everything. Especially for saving Koichi's life. I don't know what I would've done if anything happened to him."

"Just doing my job. But if it makes your life better, then I'll consider my debt to you paid."

Will shook his head. "You never owed me anything."

"I appreciate that you think so. But it still makes me feel better if something I did makes your life happier." Anthony smiled, putting little crinkles at the corners of his eyes. "Don't worry about me, Will. I'm fine. I'm seeing someone now, work's good, my life is *good*. Okay?

And now that you and I have cleared the air, I feel like I'm not holding myself back anymore. So this is good."

"Yeah."

Silence fell. Anthony started down the hallway toward the rear of the shop. Will followed. Out in the parking lot, he walked Anthony to his truck and stopped beside the driver's-side door. "So where're you going next? I'd love to keep in touch."

"Definitely." Anthony peered out over the bog. "I'll be in town for a few more days, at least. Koichi has to come in tomorrow to ID his kidnappers, if possible. You're welcome to come with him, if you like."

"I will, then." Will fished in his back pocket, pulled out one of the business cards he carried everywhere, and handed it to Anthony. "There's my cell number and email. Do keep in touch. And if you're ever back in the area, I'll take you and your boyfriend out to dinner."

"I'd like that." Anthony gazed at him with a peaceful smile. "See you in the morning, Will."

"Yeah. See you then."

Anthony opened the door and hopped into the truck. Will stood out of the way and watched until he'd driven out of sight, then went back inside. He had a phone call to make.

Koichi didn't get the call he'd expected until nearly midnight. He knew Will was alive, thanks to Agent Berry's earlier call, but he didn't know anything else, and he'd been on pins and needles ever since, waiting for Ruiz to give him the details. He snatched up the phone without looking and muted the TV in one movement. "Well? Is he okay?"

"I'm fine."

Oh my God. Will. A giant hand reached into Koichi's chest and squeezed all the blood from his heart. He curled into a ball on his sofa. "Anthony was going to call me."

"I know. I told him I wanted to do it."

Koichi's eyes stung and his throat ached. "Where are you?"

"At the shop. Anthony just left."

That felt like a kick in the chest. "Oh."

"No, Koichi. He and I needed to talk. I needed some answers. But we're not together, okay? All that was a long time ago. It's in the past. We couldn't resurrect it even if we wanted to. And neither of us wants to. Not anymore."

Something hard and tight inside Koichi let go. His vision blurred.

Will was still talking. "Anthony said you'll need to go to the police station tomorrow and ID the people who kidnapped you. I want to go with you. If you'll let me."

Koichi smiled and wiped tears from his cheeks. "That'd be awesome. Thank you."

"Hey, there's no way I'd let you face that alone."

Koichi bit a hangnail off his thumb. Watched the people on the screen argue in silence. "I'm glad you're okay, Will. I was really scared."

"Same here. I was *so* relieved to find out you were safe." The tenderness in Will's voice gave Koichi hope for the first time in days. "Good night."

"Good night."

He thumbed off his phone and slumped against the couch cushions. Relief flowed through him like waves. Whether Will shared his feelings or not, at least he didn't have to compete with Anthony the FBI hero. That was no small thing.

For the first time in days, Koichi closed his eyes and slept through the night.

His phone woke him from a dream of drowning. He clawed his way out of it and answered without looking. "Hmm?"

"Goddamn it, Chichi, you're *kidnapped* and I have to find this out from the *fucking morning news*?"

Oh. Oops. "Hi, Kimmy."

"Don't 'Hi, Kimmy' me. Explain yourself, you fucking idiot."

Hurt and fear bled through the phone, and Koichi felt like the heel he was. "I'm really sorry. I totally should've called you. It was just . . ." He trailed off, searching for the right words. There weren't any. "God, it was such a long night. They tied me up, blindfolded me, punched me in the face, threw me in a trunk, and threatened to kill me and Will. Then the FBI rescued me, and he promised to tell me if Will was okay, but he didn't call until fucking *midnight*, and I just couldn't even think of anything else, and I know I should've called but my brain was fried. I'm sorry, Kimmy. Don't hate me."

She made a soft noise. "Oh, honey. Of course I don't hate you. Are you all right? Really?"

"Yeah. I'm okay." Yawning, he pushed himself off the sofa where he'd slept the night away and switched off the TV. "Will's supposed to come over this morning and go with me to ID the assholes who kidnapped me."

"Good. I'm glad." She paused. "Does that mean you've made up?"

"I hope so." Happiness pulsed through him, suddenly, unexpectedly, bringing a wide smile to his face. "It looks like I'll probably be late today. I'm sorry."

She *pfft*ed. "Please. Don't bother coming in. I'll ask Bonnie if she can cover."

"Thanks, sis. I'll call you later, okay?"

"You better. I want all the details."

He grinned. "All of them? You sure?"

She made a gagging sound. "Okay, maybe not all. But I want the whole story from last night, and I want to know what happens with Will this morning. Promise?"

"Yeah, I promise. Love you."

"Love you too, T. Bye."

"Bye."

He ended the call and finally checked the time on his way to the kitchen. Seven fifteen. Just as well that Kimmy had woken him up. Now he had time to make coffee and shower before Will got here.

At least, he hoped so. He wasn't sure what time Will was coming over.

He sniffed his armpit and grimaced. Yikes. He definitely needed a shower. Coffee first, though. Coffee always came first.

He'd gotten the pot on, poured his first mug, and was halfway up the stairs when someone knocked on his kitchen door. Knee-jerk terror drained the strength from his legs and sent his heart leapfrogging into his throat before good sense prevailed and he realized it must be Will.

Which didn't help the shakiness and racing pulse any.

Clutching his *Torchwood* coffee mug in one hand and holding on to the stair rail for dear life with the other, he made his way back down the steps. Will's familiar silhouette stood outside the frosted glass.

For the space of a breath, Koichi stood there, shaking, remembering that he stank of old sweat and fear, that half his face was black and purple, that he wasn't wearing anything except ancient War Eagle boxer shorts with holes in them and most of the elastic gone. Then Will knocked again and laid his open palm on the glass, and none of that mattered anymore. Koichi set his coffee on the counter, hurried to the door, unlocked it, and swung it open.

CHAPTER 15

Will knew what had happened to Koichi. But it didn't prepare him for the sight of Koichi's swollen, bruised face when he opened the door.

"Oh my God." Heart aching, Will touched the enormous purple bruise spreading across Koichi's left cheek and jaw and puffing the skin around his eye. "What did they do to you?"

"They thought punching me in the face was gonna help me remember stuff I didn't know. Fucking morons." Koichi flashed the wry grin Will loved. "C'mon in. I made coffee."

He stood aside. Will walked in, watching as Koichi shut the door. He wore his favorite boxer shorts—the ones that always slipped down to show the swell of his butt—and Will saw several other bruises and a couple of small cuts on his arms, hands, and wrists. The sight of them made him want to find the people who'd done this and stomp their faces into the ground.

Koichi caught him looking. Those gorgeous green eyes softened. He skirted the table and took Will's hands in his. "How are your wrists? Are you going to be okay?"

"Yeah, it's fine. Just some scrapes, is all." They were deep. He'd done more damage than he'd intended. But technically, he was telling the truth. The doctor had said they should heal with minimal scarring.

Koichi peered at Will's bandaged wrists as if he knew it was worse than that, but didn't argue. "I'm glad you're all right. I don't know what I would've done if you'd died."

"Me too. I mean, when I found out what had happened to you . . ." His stomach churned at the memory. "I don't think I've ever been more scared in my life. But it made me realize something important."

Koichi peered at him with hope burning in his eyes. "What?"

His voice was soft. Measured. Afraid. *"I'm in love with you, Will."* Christ, was it only yesterday that Koichi had said those words, and Will had answered with uncertainty? It seemed like another lifetime.

Cupping Koichi's perfect face in his hands, Will bent and pressed a gentle kiss to his mouth. "I love you, Koichi. I'm sorry I didn't realize it before. I was so, so stupid."

Koichi's breath hitched. "Doesn't matter now. We love each other, and we're together now. And I'm not ever, ever letting you go."

Pure joy expanded in Will's chest, stopping his breath and cutting off his words. Smiling wide, he pulled Koichi close, stroking his back, kissing his hair. He thought his bliss must be shining out of him like light.

Koichi nuzzled into his neck, one hand clutching his ass. "You might've noticed I need a shower really, really bad. Want to join me?"

"Now *that* sounds like fun." He kissed Koichi again, deeper this time, and was rewarded with a breathless moan that sank into his soul like a balm. "Let's go get dirty."

Laughing, Koichi took his hand and led him upstairs.

Two hours later, Will stood beside Koichi while he peered through the two-way mirror at the five women lined up for his identification. Nothing showed on Koichi's face, but he was too pale for Will's liking, and his fingers shook in Will's grip. He rubbed his thumb over the back of Koichi's hand in soothing circles, reminding him that he wasn't alone.

"I don't know," Koichi said, finally. "I never really saw her face. Maybe if I could hear them talk?"

Anthony pushed off the wall where he'd been leaning, patiently waiting for Koichi's verdict. "Is there anything in particular that would help?"

"Um." Koichi went red and moved closer to Will, clearly embarrassed. "Maybe they could say, 'We need the pages' or something like that."

Anthony nodded. "Sure thing."

FBI. Will still had a tough time wrapping his head around that.

Anthony pushed the intercom button. "Sharon, have them all say 'We need the pages.' Okay?"

"Got it." His partner didn't seem any more fazed by the request than he did.

Some of the tightness eased from Koichi's body. But he still felt tense and nervous at Will's side. Not that anyone could blame him, after all he'd been through.

One by one, the women recited the required phrase. When the fourth one spoke, Koichi sucked in a sharp breath. After all five had finished, Anthony thanked his partner and turned to Koichi. "Did you recognize any of the voices?"

This time, he didn't hesitate. "Number four. It was her."

Will watched the woman who'd terrorized Koichi as they led her out of the little room beyond the glass. She didn't look like much— short, thin, brown hair in braids, brown eyes blinking behind square glasses. But something about her felt icy cold. He was relieved she was being locked up.

"Do I have to ID the man too?" Koichi's voice was soft and unhappy, and Will squeezed his hand. The man who'd been in the car when Anthony rescued him was dead, shot by Anthony's partner. Koichi had told Will earlier that he didn't want to identify a corpse.

Anthony studied him with a thoughtful look. "Did you see his face at any point?"

Koichi shook his head. "He punched me. That was the only contact I had with him."

"Then I don't think you can help with identification." Anthony's mouth twisted into a humorless smile. "It's sort of a moot point anyway, since our only suspect is dead."

"Good point." Koichi leaned against Will's side with a sigh. "Is this over? Do you have everybody?"

Another nod from Anthony. "We don't have our ringleader in custody yet, but we have a name, thanks to the group that had you, Will." He peered at Will with an odd look on his face. Almost sad. "I'm sorry about all this. I really am. I would've kept you out of this if I could've. I had no idea I was dragging you into my shit."

Koichi's hand tightened to the point of pain around Will's. He extricated himself and wound his arm around Koichi's shoulders, shooting him a glance that said, *Relax, I'm yours.*

"You couldn't have done anything," Will said, rubbing Koichi's arm. "It was my choice to follow you here. And I think it turned out pretty great for me, in the end." He smiled at Koichi, who beamed back at him.

"Yeah. I guess it did." Anthony eyed them both with a faint smile. "Well. In any case, I know it must've been a shock to see me in the swamp that night, with those criminals. I can imagine what you must've thought of me. I feel really bad about that."

At Will's side, Koichi shuffled foot to foot. Will pulled him closer, trying to reassure him without words. "Don't worry about it. I mean, it was surprising, yeah. But not as much as it would've been if I hadn't already seen you that other time. Not that I wasn't glad to find out you weren't involved in anything illegal, 'cause I was. I couldn't quite believe you'd gone bad."

Anthony frowned. "Wait. What other time are you talking about?"

"Huh?"

"You said you saw me in the bog another time besides when I was with the antiquities trading ring. When was that?"

"Back in April sometime. The twentieth, I think." Actually he remembered the date perfectly. It was the first time Koichi had kissed him. The first time he'd held Koichi naked in his arms and felt his body shake with pleasure. He glanced sidelong at Koichi, who favored him with a sly grin.

The expression on Anthony's face cooled the heat the memory of that night brought with it. "Will, I was never out there in April. That time you saw me with the group was the only time I ever went into the bog."

Will stared, shocked. "Are you sure?"

"Positive."

Chills crawled over Will's scalp. "But . . . but I saw you. I saw your face."

Anthony shook his head. "It wasn't me."

Then who did I see?

Will's head swam.

"Will?" Koichi rested a hand on his chest and peered up at him with brows pulled together. "You okay?"

He gave himself a mental shake. "Yeah, I'm fine."

The door to the hall opened, and Sharon walked into the room. "Suspect's in custody. Mr. McNab, we'll most likely need you to testify for the prosecution in her trial. One of us will call you with details in plenty of time for you to make arrangements."

Koichi tensed, but nodded. "Sure. You have my number."

"Thank you for coming in." Anthony held out his hand, which Koichi shook after a second's hesitation. "You've been a big help." He stuck his hands in his back pockets, a painfully familiar gesture that told Will he felt more uncomfortable than he was letting on. "It's been good to see you again, Will. Especially good to see you happy."

His throat tightened. "Good to see you too." He left it at that. There was too much else, and they'd already said everything important.

Sharon glanced between them thoughtfully, as if she sensed something was up. "You guys are free to go. Thanks for your help. We'll be in touch."

Koichi started for the door before she finished talking. "Okay. Thanks, y'all. Bye."

Will followed, led by Koichi's arm around him. He held Anthony's gaze for a second before Anthony turned away.

Be happy, Anthony.

Outside in the morning sunshine, Koichi put on his sunglasses and stretched his arms wide. "What a gorgeous day."

"It is." Will squinted upward, wishing he'd brought his shades. Wishing even more that he'd worn shorts. It was already almost ninety degrees and humid as hell. The walk back to Koichi's house wasn't far, but the damp heat here was even worse than in Houston. "What do you want to do today?"

Koichi shot him a wide smile. "Are you staying home with me?"

He nodded. "Joanie's handling the shop. I told her I needed to be with you today."

"Oh my God, that's so romantic." In the shade of a huge, Spanish-moss-hung oak, Koichi stopped, flung his arms around Will, and planted a swift kiss on his lips. "Let's go out to our spot in Hunter's Bog and fuck in your tent."

Will laughed. "I like that idea."

A mischievous grin curved Koichi's mouth. "We can do a little ghost hunting too."

Startled, Will blinked. "What?"

"C'mon. I know what you were thinking back there." Koichi pecked him on the chin, let him go, and resumed the walk home. "You thought you saw Anthony that time, but he said he wasn't there. Maybe you were imagining things, but isn't it more fun to think you saw a ghost?"

Will turned the idea over in his mind. The face he'd seen *had* been awfully pale, and very faint. He'd never found any sign of Anthony, or in fact any other person. And the bog *was* supposed to be haunted.

The memory of the shadows he'd seen during his first nights in the shop came back to him full force, along with an undeniable excitement.

"Let's do it," Will said. "The fucking *and* the ghost hunting."

Koichi took Will's hand, weaving their fingers together. He didn't say anything, but the gleam in those pretty green eyes told Will all he needed to know.

CHAPTER 16

Koichi did his best to put the whole adventure behind him. Having Will in his life made it easier. The fact that Will had suffered the same sort of trauma brought them even closer, though Koichi wished like hell that Will hadn't had to go through that. Still, six weeks and four days after their reconciliation, he was deliriously happy, and he felt confident in saying Will was too.

The only fly in his personal ointment was the damn journal pages. The journal itself hadn't been recovered yet. Neither had his grandmother's perfume bottle or jewelry. Anthony had told him it was unlikely they would ever get any of it back, but they'd keep trying. Koichi had pretty much resigned himself to the loss. But he couldn't let go of the idea of finding the missing pages.

Will laughed when Koichi brought it up for at least the millionth time while they were having a rare night out at the fancy new restaurant in Spanish Fort. "Come on, T. When are you going to let that go?"

"I don't see why I should. The journal was supposed to lead to Severin Lamar's stolen jewels. If those thieves wanted the missing pages that badly, it must be the part with the details about where the jewels were hidden." Koichi scraped the last of his crawfish gumbo out of the bowl with the crust of bread he'd saved for that purpose. "Aren't you even a little bit curious?" He crammed the gumbo and bread into his mouth and chewed, watching Will's face.

"Well, yeah, but . . ." Will's grin faded. "You almost died because of those pages, Koichi. No matter how curious I might be, that sours the whole thing for me."

Koichi's heart lurched. Reaching across the table, he took Will's hand in his. "I think about that too. How those pieces of shit nearly killed you because of that stupid journal. But we're alive, Will. And I can't help but think that whole business might be part of what brought us back together."

The lips Koichi loved to kiss curved into a smile. "You could be right."

He smiled back. "In any case, wouldn't it be just the best *fuck you* ever if we found those pages and got the jewels, while those assholes are rotting in prison?"

Will laughed again, brown eyes shining in the candlelight. "That's why I love you. Your very special sense of revenge."

"I thought you loved me for my body."

"That too."

Sweet warmth bubbled up inside Koichi, leaving him light and joyful. He leaned over the small table, gazing into Will's expressive face. "Whether we find those pages or not, whether we find the jewels or not, we found each other. That's all the treasure I really need." He squeezed Will's hand, still clasped in his. "I love you more than anything, and I'm not ever letting you go."

The humor sparkling in Will's eyes softened into a familiar tenderness. "I love you too."

They didn't kiss, since this wasn't the place for it. But they didn't need to. They knew each other's hearts and minds well enough.

Sitting back in his chair, Koichi picked up his wineglass and sipped from it. Studying Will's face, Koichi saw none of the sad, haunted look from when they'd first met. Instead, he saw a man at peace. A man whose personal ghosts had finally been vanquished.

A happy man. As happy as he's made me.

He lifted his glass in a silent toast. Will mirrored the movement, and they grinned at one another.

Yeah. Life was good.

Dear Reader,

Thank you for reading Ally Blue's *The Secret of Hunter's Bog*!

We know your time is precious and you have many, many entertainment options, so it means a lot that you've chosen to spend your time reading. We really hope you enjoyed it.

We'd be honored if you'd consider posting a review—good or bad—on sites like **Amazon, Barnes & Noble, Kobo, Goodreads, Twitter, Facebook, Tumblr**, and your blog or website. We'd also be honored if you told your friends and family about this book. Word of mouth is a book's lifeblood!

For more information on upcoming releases, author interviews, blog tours, contests, giveaways, and more, please sign up for our weekly, spam-free newsletter and visit us around the web:

Newsletter: tinyurl.com/RiptideSignup
Twitter: twitter.com/RiptideBooks
Facebook: facebook.com/RiptidePublishing
Goodreads: tinyurl.com/RiptideOnGoodreads
Tumblr: riptidepublishing.tumblr.com

Thank you so much for Reading the Rainbow!

RiptidePublishing.com

ALSO BY ALLY BLUE

For a complete booklist, please visit www.allyblue.com.

ABOUT THE AUTHOR

Ally Blue is acknowledged by the world at large (or at least by her heroes, who tend to suffer a lot) as the Popess of Gay Angst. She has a great big suggestively shaped hat and rides in a bullet-proof Plexiglas bubble in Christmas parades. Her harem of manwhores does double duty as bodyguards and inspirational entertainment. Her favorite band is Radiohead, her favorite color is lime green, and her favorite way to waste a perfectly good Saturday is to watch all three extended-version LOTR movies in a row. Her ultimate dream is to one day ditch the evil day job and support the family on manlove alone. She is not a hippie or a brain surgeon, no matter what her kids' friends say.

Website: allyblue.com
Facebook profile: facebook.com/AllyBlue.author
Facebook fan page: facebook.com/pages/Ally-Blue/98548113963
Twitter: twitter.com/PopessAllyBlue
Pinterest: pinterest.com/popessallyblue/
Tumblr: therealallyblue.tumblr.com
Yahoo group: groups.yahoo.com/neo/groups/loveisblue/info
Goodreads: goodreads.com/author/show/34997.Ally_Blue